Another Night

For Belle MacIntyre

who persisted

Another NIGHT

Cape Breton Stories True & Short & Tall

EDITED WITH AN INTRODUCTION BY RONALD CAPLAN

Breton Books
Wreck Cove, Cape Breton Island
1995

The stories in **Another Night** originally appeared in *Cape Breton's Magazine*. Ruth Holmes Whitehead shared with us the pleasure of interviewing Max Basque. The text of "The Yarning Old Men of Strawberry Glen" came from Beaton Institute, University College of Cape Breton. The English translation is by Norman MacDonald, a native of Skye then teaching in Cape Breton. Sid Timmons' stories are edited from tapes collected by Brian Sutcliffe, as part of research toward a CBC Cape Breton broadcast, "Remember the Miner." Linda MacLellan of Belle Côte collected the stories told by Archie Neil Chisholm.

Another Night is part of the Large Print Program of the National Library of Canada.

Production Assistance: Bonnie Thompson
Transcription: Glenda Watt and Wendy Wishart

Breton Books
Wreck Cove, Cape Breton Island
Nova Scotia B0C 1H0

Canadian Cataloguing in Publication Data
Main entry under title:

Another night
  ISBN 1-895415-01-2

1. Tales — Nova Scotia — Cape Breton Island.
I. Caplan, Ronald, 1942-

GR113.5.C36A66 1994 398.2'09716'9 C95-950009-X

Editor's Introduction
by Ronald Caplan

Since the publication of **Cape Breton Book of the Night (Tales of Tenderness & Terror)**, readers have asked me whether I had enough Cape Breton stories for another book. The simple answer to that is that there seems to be no end to them, and I keep gathering more. Johnny Murphy, explaining his room full of unusual musical instruments, once told me that "if you take an interest in something, it will come to you." In any case, life goes on in Cape Breton and people here continue to talk with one another, and to talk with me. And the storymaking process is an ongoing part of that talk.

If you ask about the weather or directions on the street, you rarely get a one-sentence answer. Your question has so many connections. There is the tendency to want to hold you, to see you as an audience and company, even for a few minutes—perhaps even see you as a source. There seems to be a felt responsibility to give you more than you asked for—about the sweetest kind of value-added I know. To give you more than you asked for and to do it well, as perhaps their mother or father would have done, taking the time, and making your day. And proving once again, as some people so often say the first few times the visitor tries to get up and go home: "Oh, you've got plenty of time."

What I like especially in **Another Night** is that, in this mix of stories, we can see storymaking-in-progress—general conversation being honed by re-telling, the experience and art of one person becoming part of the repertoire and responsibility of the person who has heard the story. I love to think of it as re-creation—as *significantly* passing the time—making something new and more and connected and a joy in the world, no matter how hard or funny or frightening the story.

Which is not to suggest that **Another Night** was collected casually, out of the run of daily lives that include tales of giants and riding on the eagle's back. People in Cape Breton rarely tell you a story like that when you stop them for directions. Although they are liable to tell you about the huge tuna caught by men who went out after tiny mackerel, or the year they brought an entire winter's wood down off the mountain in a couple of minutes. On the other hand, there are people here who, once they realize you're a stranger, will tell you that you had better come home for a cup of tea—and after they've got you to help them bring in wood or turn part of a field of hay or just admire their garden—and after the "tea" has turned into more of a meal than you could ever hope to finish—*then* there is no telling the direction stories might take, yours or theirs, from recent incidents to a tale "my father told right at this table I don't know how many times"—of the devil, or giants, or riding on great birds.

For over 20 years I've lived in Cape Breton, making my living publishing *Cape Breton's Magazine*—which means travelling the island with a tape recorder and camera, gathering what I can and returning it to the community. Sometimes I knew in general the story I was going for and more often I didn't. Sometimes I would go looking for the history of life in the Clyburn Valley before farms there became a golf course, and I'd come away with a sweet story of treasure and love. Sometimes all I got was the conversation.

Cape Breton Book of the Night was a collection of stories that touched more on the supernatural. **Another Night** contains a few of that kind of story, but my interest here was to bring together more of the range of Cape Breton storytelling. Actually, **Another Night** is not quite accurate. This book might have been called "Other Nights," and "Afternoons," and even "the Occasional Morning"—anytime people will sit with me and pass the time.

Stories survive because people tell them. Over and over Silver Donald Cameron reminds me that mediums might change but the "appetite for story" continues to be strong. And Joe Neil MacNeil, a beloved Cape Breton Gaelic storyteller, likes to remind me of the setting in which story most matters to him: "There has be a voice that says the words and an ear to receive it—otherwise there's no connection." Again and again, I think of Theresa Curtis MacDonald's little soft outcry regarding her family and the long story-songs they shared: "Oh," she said, "the time we had for one another!" All of which reminds me of our responsibility for so fragile an item as story and the act of storymaking. It also reminds me that we get the world we want only because we make it happen....

Which is to say that it delights me when people stop me to tell me a story and I realize that they learned it from something I collected, that they are determined to keep it alive and to pass it along. It is not the traditional setting: it includes a fellow from Away with a tape recorder, mid-afternoon in the evening of the storyteller's life rather than night during the storyteller's more vigorous years, but I hope portions of **Another Night** will cling to your heart and find expression the next time someone stops you for direction, or asks the time.

Ronald Caplan
Wreck Cove
1994

Contents

Another Night

How the Two Bulls Went to Orangedale

told by Alfred P. MacKay

Well, there's really two bulls in the story.

The first fellow, he was on tether out there in the field. And I was oystering at that time of the year. But anyway, my father, he informed me that I would have to do something with the bull. That he was sick and tired of pulling him around on a tether, you know. And that Jack Munro (the butcher) would buy him, if I took him to Orangedale. So, okay. I said, "Tomorrow, I'll do it." So, I went....

It took all day.

And there was a fellow up the road here, he was a young fellow. He was teaching school—we had a school here. And he went to the road with me and helped me get the rope on the bull. And then he went to the school.

And of course, the bull took off the first thing. At the tide gallop, out that wood road was there. He took off. He went out. And *he* was the boss on the rope, you know. I couldn't hold him. He went that way till I got a turn (of the rope around) a tree, somewhere out there. And then he didn't want to come back. And he lay down, and he wouldn't get up. And I had to break off limbs and start a fire under his head, you know. (*Really? You started a little fire under his head!*) Oh, yes. And

1

he didn't get up. And I couldn't see him; it was smoking. And all of a sudden he got up with one spring. But he was choking with the smoke, you know. They were contrary, animals like that.

(*And you weren't afraid of him.*) No. I wasn't afraid of him. But I wasn't supposed to hammer him, neither. His meat would be, you know—he was on his way to be killed. And if you pound him and bruise him all up, why his carcass wouldn't be fit. You'd get nothing for it. A blow will show on an animal. It'll show terrible on the meat.

(*So you couldn't be too rough on him.*) No.

And when I got back in to the main road, still at the schoolhouse here—recess was on—it was quarter to eleven. Kids were out having recess.

So I started. I still had to take her to Orangedale, see. Up the road. It was 14 or 15 miles, you know, on the feet.

I'd never have done it, only for the telephone. (*Telephone?*) Well, the posts. (*Oh, the telephone poles!*) It was a new line; it was up there solid as could be. And when he'd go the way of Orangedale, we were making 15 or 20 miles an hour. He'd be on the tide gallop, see? And I would hang on just until my last breath was leaving me, and (then) I'd take a turn (around) the post. And (the rope would) fetch up. And it would put him right flat on his back. That was taking the conceit out of him. After awhile, he wouldn't run, you know. But he could never figure out what was knocking him. That took the conceit out of him.

Because the only way he'd go—he'd stand. Till I'd set fire to him or something. And then he'd take off, as hard as he could gallop. And I had a good rope on him, see. And I'd let him go, and me after him, hard as I could go. And when I knew I was going to give up the ghost, I'd take a turn on a telephone pole. And of course, you could just see him make a somersault and fetch up, you know! Land on his back. After awhile...he seemed to get wise a little bit! By that time I got going to Orangedale pretty good.

Every queer thing happened, you know. At Crowdis Bridge, there was a car burning on the middle of the road. Well now, I had a big job to put a bull by that, you know. And there wasn't a soul there, just the car burning. And I found out afterwards, there were fellows came up fishing trout. And the finance company was going to take the car. They set fire to it and went back to Sydney some other way. Let it burn there, see.

But the evening train at five o'clock— Express used to be going to Sydney—she passed me. I was *still* a mile from Orangedale.

But I got into Orangedale. And when I got there, I put him in John Hughie's barn. John Hughie MacDonald—his barn was below the station. Put it in there, and I turned and walked home.

And this little hill up here, up the road about a half a mile from here—I fell on the hill. Walked backing up. Not ate a bite all day. And I fell asleep. And I just caught myself, and jumped up-

3

right. "First thing I'll be here all night asleep!" I was feeling lively, and I was that tired I could sleep right there. I made home, anyway.

So the next year, another bull. But I took him over to the shore here, and we put him in a big rowboat we had. (*Put him in the rowboat?*) Yeah. I knocked him. I was pretty smart then. I had him by the two horns. I twisted his head so much that he fell. And then there was a fellow with me. I tied the bull's one front leg and the hind leg together on one side, and the same on the other. And took the boat sideways to the shore. And rolled him in it. And went to Orangedale.

Was one hour I was in Orangedale! Cut the bull loose and let him go. Ronald MacInnes hollered from over here—he was standing at the store, and it was right near to the shore, you know. "I never seen it before," he said, "a bull coming in a boat!"

(*That's a dandy story.*) I should have made a good movie, you know! I don't know how it would look but I know—oh, boy, I was really a-flying. I could run fast, you know. And I'm sure I looked happy, because he was going the way I wanted to go. I never tried to stop him when he was going that way. If I'd play out, though, you know—I had to take care of myself—then I'd never be able to finish the trip. So I'd have to put the brakes on the thing, you know, before I'd get played out so bad that I couldn't look after him.

4

(Oh, you did it like an athlete. But afterwards, you just about fell asleep on the road.) After walking 30 miles then, when I was getting nearly home. Nothing to eat. Not a thing, you know, I didn't have anything. *(You didn't take a lunch.)* No, no, no. I never thought I'd be that long. I thought I'd make it in two or three hours, you know!... And after a month, my father got $12. That's the time I put him on the road. So I earned that $12! The time I put him on the road. Took me all day, fighting him on the road. *(Your father got the $12.)* Oh, yes. *(And did he give it to you?)* Oh, no! I didn't expect it! He was running the ranch then, you know. I was only a little hired man.

The Port Hood Explosion

told by Amelia Cook

February 7th, 1908. Really and truly, I was only five years old, but I kind of believe it was a Wednesday. I'm not sure. But I remember it so well because that morning the wind was in east and there were great big flakes of snow—Cape Breton snowflakes are bigger than around here (in Guysborough Town)—they were awfully big, any-

5

way, big as the palm of your hand. You've seen that wet snow. And it filled the window all full of blisters—we used to call it blisters—covered with snow on the window.

How I remember so well, Daddy went to work that morning and Mama had a big washing out, and the wind came in and blew all the clothes off the line. She said to me, "Amelia, I've got to go out and pick them up." It wasn't daylight yet. She took the table and she pushed it over by the window and put the lamp on it so she could see outdoors to pick up her clothes—they blew all over the place. I kept watching her and watching her, and after awhile she came in. I shouldn't tell you this, probably—but she had Daddy's underclothes. And years ago, you know, there were no combinations—there were just drawers and shirts—they were froze.... She'd spread them apart and they'd stand up. She spread the drawers' legs apart like that and said, "Look, Amelia, a man with no head on him." And I remember that as well as anything. Anything to make us laugh.

Then she moved the table to the next window and went out to pick up more clothes. They were even stuck against the wire fence of the railroad. And it was snowing. And she just got in, started putting the clothes in the tub to thaw out, and this tap came on the window—and here it was Joe Porter, our next-door neighbour.

It was about seven o'clock then. I can see that big grey mitt in the window. He pulled the

6

snow down off the window—and he said, "Laura, Laura, there's an explosion in the pit and it's on Da's side. I'm going over to tell Nell."

Mama said, "You stay here. You go over and tell Nell, she'll want to go to the pit. They've got trouble enough at the pit."

But Mama couldn't keep him. Over he goes and boy, it wasn't two minutes or probably a little more, over comes Nell in her cotton nightdress and her bare feet in that deep snow—she was going to the pit. Poor Mama had an awful time trying to get her peacified to stay.

So a little after daylight one of our neighbours went on horseback to the pit, and he came back and told Mama that Mr. Peterson (Amelia's father) and Mr. Porter were all right—because they were shifted. When they went to work that morning, Papa was transferred to another place—him and Tom Porter—three of them were to be working together, the two and this John Campbell. The explosion went off on the side Daddy was supposed to be on, but just this day he was on the other side of the pit. That's how he and Tom Porter got saved.

But poor Daddy, when he was getting out of the rake that morning, he said to John Campbell, "I'll see you tonight, John." And John said, "All right, Alex, I'll see you tonight." And Papa said, when he got back to the explosion, the first man he picked up was John Campbell. And he had his (lunch) can still over his shoulder. And Papa said,

7

first thing he thought of, "I'll see you tonight, John."

When the explosion went off, Daddy laid down. And they say the gas lays about two or three feet from the bottom—it goes in a ball like—and a certain distance from the top—and Daddy laid down and the gas went over him. But there were scorches on Daddy's coat just the same. But he was handy enough to the surface to get out. Daddy sent word home that he was all right but that he was staying behind to help the men. Then he went back in the mine—and that's when he found John Campbell. Nearly killed Daddy. It broke his heart.

(*What caused the explosion?*) These poor Bulgarians. The boys used to tease them because they talked different and everything. Used to steal their picks and powder and all this. And they had the open teapot lamps in those days, used to have the flame on their heads. And the poor Bulgarians, they used to hide their tools in behind a brattice. Well, there was a pocket of gas behind the brattice this day, and when the examiner was looking for gas, he didn't find it—but whenever the Bulgarians went into that little cubbyhole, their lamps lit the pocket of gas.

There were ten men killed—some of them Bulgarians. And Papa and Mama always said that they don't think that those Bulgarian wives ever found out whatever happened to their husbands—because nobody knew their addresses, nobody

8

knew the place they were really from, any more than they knew they were Bulgarians. Papa and Mama always said there was money there for their widows.

But they're buried in Port Hood in the Catholic graveyard. (*Were they buried in the graveyard right away?*) No. My Daddy and some more of our neighbours were seeing about getting them buried. And Papa said to them, "I want to have those men buried in the Catholic cemetery." And they said to him, "Well, how do you know they're Catholic?" "Well," Papa said, "they are, they bless themselves." "Well, how many fingers do they use to bless themselves?" Papa said they blessed themselves with two fingers, anyway. Papa was getting pretty mad. And they told Papa, "Well, if it was only two fingers, they were a *sort* of a Protestant."

That made Papa awful mad. And he made a jump for the fellow, but they held him back. Papa was an awful good man, and everybody that knew him always gave him a great name—but he didn't like that because it bothered him to think, you know, the men were dead, and nobody to fight for them or their rights—and Daddy was a Protestant. And when they said, "Well, they're sort of a Protestant..."—that got Daddy mad. Daddy was Church of England. Daddy wouldn't bury them in the Protestant ground, no sir. Daddy said to them, "They're Catholic, and they're going to be buried in a Catholic ground."

Anyhow, they buried the four Bulgarians outside the fence of the Catholic graveyard. Then they wrote to the Pope, in Rome I suppose, and when they got the message back from the Pope, he said they were Catholic people, all right—that the Bulgarians as a rule were of the Catholic faith. And they didn't dig them up as they do today. They put the fence out around them.

Editor's Note: Newspapers called the explosion the worst disaster in Inverness County history. They listed the dead as Malcolm Beaton, John Lauchie Gillis, John T. Campbell, Duncan McDonald, Allan R. McDonald, William McKenzie and Four Bulgarians, "names unknown," part of a party of twenty in the country only about two months.

"But we went out after mackerel...!"

told by Merrill MacInnis

We went out that morning to catch mackerel just for filleting for the winter—we were going to salt them. And we were all through crab fishing. Had taken all our crab gear ashore, and we just wanted to get some extra fish for the winter. For pickling. And we went out, I guess, seven o'clock or so. Charlie was with me—Charlie MacAskill. And we were out there around 10:00, I guess. And we had caught a couple of hundred pounds of mackerel, so we thought, Well, that will do for today. We'll come in and fillet them, and get home by lunchtime.

So it was 10:30. We had come up to the bell buoy—up by the harbour up here (at Little River)—and we started cleaning the mackerel. We had done, oh, maybe half of them, filleted them. And we had a whole bunch of seagulls—about a hundred seagulls—they were just sitting down getting the trimmings of the mackerel. And just all of a sudden like somebody fired a rifle, the hundred seagulls just went phroop!—took right off to the air. And Charlie said, "What the hell happened to the seagulls?" I figured maybe the bilge pump had come on and it just stirred the water— beautiful day, calm day, you know. And then, a

11

few of the seagulls came back. And the next thing—Jesus, they took off again. And there was this great big wake in the water. Like something had come up to the surface.

So I looked at Charlie and he was looking at me by this time, and we said, "What in the hell was that?!" So we got suspicious then. So I threw another piece of mackerel out—and up came this gigantic fish. And we could just see sort of the top of him. So I leaned down over the side of the boat—and it looked like a sturgeon. We'd catch them in the salmon net, when my father and I had the nets out. And he had the colour and stuff of the sturgeon. I was sure that's what it was. But I thought he looked an awful unusually big.

So I said, "Oh, boy, we should try throwing another piece of fish out—see if he'll come back again." So we threw the fish out. And this time he came—about half of him came out of the water. I knew for sure what we had then.

So here was this gigantic tuna. And you could see his eye. That was the first thing you'd see coming—great big eye heading right for you. And as soon as I saw what it was, my hands were tied—there was nothing I could do. I wasn't legally allowed to fish them. I don't have a licence to fish them.

So I ran up to the cabin and called Minerva (Merrill's wife)—we have the C. B. (Citizens' Band radio). And I said, "Get ahold of Lloyd right quick." (Lloyd is Merrill's brother.)

And everything just fell into place. Happened to be someone there that day. Otherwise she couldn't leave the baby—the baby was in bed. I told her to call Lloyd on the telephone. There was no answer there. So I said, "You better go and get him. We have about a 700- or 800-pound tuna floating around the boat."

So she took off over to Lloyd's. He was out back. And Lloyd started up in the truck, and he had a radio in the truck. He got talking to me in the boat, asking if the fish was still there. And there were other boats out jigging that day. And they heard what was going on. Dennis Smith was one of them. And Dennis was going in the harbour just as Lloyd was coming up to the shore. Lloyd's boat was out on the collar; it was tied out on anchor. Dennis said, "When you get to the wharf, just jump in my boat and I'll take you out to your boat." And there happened be an agricultural representative, Mike Johnson from Truro visiting that day—so he came along with Lloyd for the drive. When they got there, Big Alex (Matheson) was on the wharf. So the three of them—Mike, Big Alex, and Lloyd—took off.

So half an hour after I made the first call on the radio, Lloyd was out alongside us.

But all this time, we were feeding the fish. And it was just perfect. You'd have the big head at the top and just the backbone—it would float on top of the water—and he'd come up and he'd just grab the head—just every one of them. Sometimes he'd do a little roll over. And we tried dropping them just two inches away from the side of the boat, and he'd come right up alongside the boat. You could even feel the boat rocking from the turbulence from him. Oh, it was amazing. Even to experience that was quite a thrill. Even if you never even thought of catching him, you know.

When Lloyd got there—by this time we had finished cleaning all the fish so we had no fish trimmings left to feed him. So we tried feeding the fillets. It was all trimmings we were feeding him up until Lloyd got there. And there were guys calling me on the radio: "We have lots of mackerel if you want us to come over with them." And I thought if they would come over that they might scare him. I said, "No. You better stay away."

So we kept feeding him the fillets. And Lloyd got there. And we saved two whole fish, so that he'd have them for the hooks. He had all the gear all ready to go on the boat. (*Lloyd has the license.*) Oh, yeah. And he had the gear on the boat in case he would see one during crab fishing.

The first thing he put out was an artificial squid. And for some reason the fish—he knew there was something different going on. He wouldn't come up near as high to the surface. Whether it was because of this artificial squid or was it because of the different colour bottom— Lloyd had a different colour bottom on his boat. But he didn't seem to want to come up near as high. And it was only once in a while. And we

14

thought, Well, this is it, you know, we're just not going to.

So then, we had the two boats alongside each other. We gave Lloyd another mackerel. On another hook. And he put the mackerel over. And on the end of this line there was a steel cable first, and then a quarter-inch rope with 600 feet of play on it and a buoy on the end of it. So this time he came up and he took the baited hook—and he went. Soon as he did, he just darted. Soon as he got ahold of the hook in his mouth.

And I'm telling you, he went. And he headed for deep water. We just let the 600 feet go in a matter of seconds. The buoy went out in the water—it's one of those big red balls—and there was spray coming from it. He was almost dragging the ball under. Just incredible. I doubt if we could have kept up to him with the boat.

So we kept an eye contact on the ball all the time. He kept going and going and going—just like hell out for deep water. Then after about half an hour you could see that he was slowing down. And we were just hyper by this time. We knew then that we had him. We were quite sure that he was hooked for good.

It was twelve o'clock, exactly, that we hooked him. And after forty-five minutes he started really slowing down. He kept going. And after an hour or an hour and fifteen minutes, he used to stop. And he'd stop for five minutes, then he'd go really fast for ten minutes, then he'd stop for three or four—

and each time it was getting longer and longer and longer. And finally at 2:30, he finally stopped. And we thought, He's ready to haul in now.

And we were quite a ways out here—it's still a nice day on the water—and Charlie and I were still in my boat, and Lloyd and Mike and Alex were in Lloyd's—so we decided we better all go in one boat and try and take him in. And Charlie and I jumped in the boat. I left the boat out there. And when I think of it afterwards, I never even thought of putting an anchor out, nothing—just jumped in the boat and left her in the middle of the ocean, floating around, ready for salvage.

So we took the buoy—grabbed ahold of it—and he took off with it again. We thought we should leave it for a little while yet. And he stopped again. And there was no movement whatsoever in him. So we started hauling him in. And we decided it would be just one person that would haul on the rope because we were scared that the hook, if we pulled too hard, that we might pull the hook out. I got hold of the quarter-inch rope, and I was pulling it in— maybe thirty feet of it in—and he'd go with ten of it. Then I'd pull another forty or fifty—just all of a sudden he'd just take off with maybe thirty feet of it. And there was no way you could hold it.

And it was forty-five minutes from the time I started pulling the rope to the time we saw him alongside the boat. He came up right alongside. And there was still a little bit of life in him. We put a dart in him to make sure that we wouldn't lose him. (That gave us) another rope—we were able to pull him up even more. And we got a big rope in through his mouth. We were hoping to get him in, take him into the boat.

There were five of us. And with the exception of Charlie, I'm sure each one of us weighed over 220 pounds. And Alex was like over 300. And we were just huffing and puffing, boy, for all that was in us. We couldn't budge him. Just couldn't do a thing with him. We hooked up the trap hauler and we put a derrick on it—and we just couldn't budge him. We decided then that we'd tow him in.

And it was funny, you know, all this time, like we were making guess on the weight—but I never once thought all the time that we were doing it—until it hit me when we were coming in the harbour: I thought "Holy God, that fish is worth like $4.00 a pound." And here's a $4000 fish coming in behind the boat. And it was the first time that I'd even clicked that the thing was worth anything. All the time we were out there, from 10:30 in the morning to this must have been 3:30 in the afternoon—it never entered my mind that the fish was worth much. (*And how much was the mackerel worth?*) Oh, fifteen cents a pound or something.

It ended up the fish was worth $5121. It weighed 1029 pounds. And we got $5.00 a pound for it.

But that was the most exciting day I ever had in my life on the water, I'll tell you. Just incredible.

Bill Daye's Woodpecker Friend

There's another little story here, too, a very strange incident. One time I used to go down around South Bar along the shore for a walk. In the fields back of there, there were all kinds of birds. And I was up through the fields, and this little woodpecker was crawling around, flying around in the grass, a little red-headed woodpecker—he had a broken leg. So I picked him up, I took him home. I made splints and put them on his leg. I kept him quite awhile, a few months. I had a hell of a job finding flies and bugs for him all the time. So anyway, I had him, and he got along well. So I took him back to the woods again, in the spot where I found him, and I said, He'll be all right.

So a few days after that, I was coming down Broadway—that would be a good quarter of a mile, a half a mile from where I had found the bird—I was coming down the street, and this bird dropped in front of me on the street. I picked him up—he was quiet—and here was my woodpecker that I had fixed his leg. He knew me from wherever he saw, and he came to me.

Later on that summer I was out on a raft, diving and swimming, me and Frank MacKillop, out up the shore at South Bar. And this bird struck the raft and fell in the water. Frank grabbed him quick—"I got a bird, I got a bird!" I

18

said, "Listen, that's my woodpecker." I took him, and it *was* my woodpecker. However he saw me and recognized me out there with a bathing suit on—he must have known my voice.

So I took him again and I took him back to the woods. And I've never encountered him any more. But I never knew that a bird had vision so good, or could remember a person or like a person so much. He appreciated so much what I'd done for him that he became my best friend, as far as birds go.

Amelia Cook's Pig

Oh, the steamers—did I love them! Different coal boats—oh, there'd be four or five laying in there at a time, waiting for coal. Big black steamers with a red bottom on them. Were they ever lovely! I can see them up there yet. And where that pier was, today that's filled in. People are picking cranberries right where the boats landed coal. And the band would play at night on those steamers. It was just a band among themselves, aboard the steamer—and it would kind of drift across the waves—would it ever be nice. Oh, talk. We had an old pig. And whenever that band would play, the old pig would run and he'd jump and he'd play back and forth. Daddy thought there was something wrong with him. He wrote into *Family Herald* to find out what they had to say about it. And they said, no, it wasn't going to hurt the pig. A lot of people thought he was crazy, when he'd hear the music—it'd go right to his heart.

Bill Forbrigger's Cure

My father and I, and my brother, the oldest fellow, were beating up the Lake.... So he took the toothache. Oh good God, he was going right crazy with the toothache—ready to jump overboard. So my father took a nail and he pointed it, and told him to pick his gums with it till it bled. And go ashore and drive it in a tree that he thought would never be cut down. So I rowed him ashore—he was screaming. And he drove it in a tree. And on the way back, he was laughing. Toothache left him just like that. And the tooth all went to pieces and fell out. They won't believe that.

My father also gave him a little prayer to say—but I never heard what the prayer was. I tried the same thing at Point Tupper, with a nail and a great big old tree we had there—I knew it would never be cut down. At that time, anyway. So I picked my tooth, and picked it, got it full of blood, and I drove it in the tree. But I think it made it worse!... Didn't know the prayer, no.

How We Got the Sheep off Bird Islands

told by Daniel John Campbell

Sheep were kept on the inside island. The New Campbellton people put sheep out there. Pasture all summer. Shear them and put them out on the island. Quite a number of years. Those islands were wooded away back. The outside island, the trees went to boat building and firewood. The inside island, it's only ten years the last clump of trees died off. Was quite a shelter there for the sheep. But when the sheep left that island, the birds took over and they sat in those trees and that's what killed the trees—cormorants. Spruce will stand a lot, but it won't stand rich ground.

Anyway, Malcolm MacDermid had an old sheep, she went out year after year with the rest of them. And that sheep got that wise, when they'd be taking them off in the fall, she'd lead the rest of the sheep down.

See, the lambs would get wild through the summer—they're hard to round up. The men would go out there—the old sheep would be down on the rocks waiting for them. They'd usually pick a fine day and they could lay the boat close to the rocks. You can herd sheep in a boat, you know; get one sheep started and they'll all follow. But this old sheep would lead them down. She'd stand to one side and the rest of them start jumping in the boat. And when that old sheep figured there was enough in the boat, she'd cut the line off. They'd go with that boat and bring another one in. That's a pretty wise old sheep now.

I kept sheep on the island. And it was worthwhile keeping them out there. The only trouble with sheep on the island, if you didn't get the lambs at the right time they'd be too heavy for market. People wouldn't believe you were selling lamb. They thought it was sheep. They'd do that well. Wonderful pasture there....

One year, we also put a heifer out there— about a year and a half heifer. And that was a wild fall. Storm after storm. We'd usually get the sheep off the island in October—never later than early November if we could. One storm after the other. Just couldn't settle down. Sea on the shores, too hard to come off. And in December—back about 1940—Wally MacKenzie, my brother-in-law, and I took off for the island.

Wally was no seaman but a pretty good butcher. The plan was: butcher the heifer. And butcher some of the lambs, if necessary. And take the sheep ashore alive. Had a little motorboat. It was after a heavy rainstorm.

Morning looked pretty good. I was after Father to let me go long before that. "No, the weather wouldn't be fit."

So this day, decided to get out and round them up fast. "It will be coming nor'west, boy. Better make it in the day because it'll be coming nor'west before too long."

Started out for the island. Had a bit of a sail I carried on the boat. And when we got to Cape Dauphin it came across nor'west. Didn't think much of it. Fresh breeze. I put the sail on her. And before we got to the harbour it had the sail off her, blowing a gale nor'west.

Square away and managed to land her at the harbour—good slip there that time. You could go in on the slip or you could go round around the harbour and go in on the sloping rock. You wouldn't call it a harbour. But anyway, decided to put it on the rocks. Slip wasn't too good. Gave Wally the oar, to back water on the oar and try to round her around and get her up on the rock. There was a danger if you missed the rock: you'd go in between the rock and the island, go out and pound on the rocks, could get damaged. Anyway, managed to get her up on the rock. Ordinary weather she'd be okay. Leave her there for weeks. But a northeast heavy storm, of course, you had to get it off the rock. Sea'll wash over that rock.

Anyhow, we rounded up the sheep. And boy, it came in northeast in the evening. Had them all rounded up, had them corralled in the barn. Had to get the boat off the rock. Couldn't load the sheep in that weather. Put the boat over on the slipway. Haul her up high.

It blew for two or three days. We were there three nights. One wild northeast snowstorm. And froze. This is in December. Turned cold. That island iced up clean to the grass. Every rock had a quarter inch of ice on it. And that's what we were in.

The second evening, we were listening to the news in the evening, after trying to get ourselves out of the harbour that day—soaked to the hide. We could have got out all right, I think, but scared we'd perish before we got in—so cold, so wet. And this news flash came over: "If Daniel Campbell and Wally MacKenzie are alive on Bird Island, put up a flare."

Well, I was expecting it. I ran off five gallons of kerosene. I grabbed an old coat hanging in the lighthouse, got up on the island, put it on the grass and poured the five gallons of kerosene. And lit her up. Took off in the gale of wind like a flare. They saw it in here and knew we were alive.

And the next day Father and Uncle John and Jimmy Carey arrived. Jimmy Carey had the biggest boat around here that time. I saw them coming, hauled our boat up, took the engine out of her and turned her bottom up—I figured I may not get back any more this winter. They came to the south side of the island. I tied a rope and slid down, and Father came in in the dory they had in tow. I had already butchered everything, and we wanted to get the meat off. Butchered the whole works. Figured that was the wise thing to do. Otherwise, might have to leave them there all winter.

They went to a flat rock up the other end of the island from the harbour. You couldn't land the dory—a ledge of rock straight down—but we lugged all that meat up. I was a young able man then. Carried all that meat up about a half mile, packed on our backs, trip after trip, while they steamed around. They anchored the boat and came in in the dory, rocking back and forth in the surf, and we'd drop a quarter of lamb down on a rope. Got all the meat down that way. Slide the meat down on the ice. Worked out all right. Then Wally went down. Then I slid down the rope last. And the rope was there till the next spring.

"On my own land!"
told by Alex Storm

You know, I bought a piece of land on Havenside (in Louisbourg)—just a barren piece of land. There were no French constructions or anything on it. I decided to test the ground, see what it was like— perhaps build a summer cottage. So around '70 or '71 I dug on that land to see where the bedrock would start.

I dug a trench across it, and that trench is still there today. And lo and behold, when I reached about a foot, foot and a half down—there was an unusual big square block of granite laying there. And I almost got vibes, that this didn't belong there.

I was digging around that rock and I found a human skeleton—old and brittle, just falling apart. I thought, oh my god, it may be some old grave site. I tried to gather all these bones up and put them in a little box and reburied them. I found with that body many small cannonballs, clusters of them.

You know, you read of guys digging up skeletons that they shouldn't be digging up, and hearing noises in the night—well, I never had a run-in with that sort of thing. But I had a bloody nightmare—a real bloody nightmare—about the guy who this skeleton belonged to. I dreamt that this guy was aboard of a ship, and he was at odds with his captain—it was an old sixteenth-century ship. And I dreamt that he was standing in the grand cabin, arguing to high heaven with his captain, and that his captain did away with him and buried him there. And all that time I was a sort of witness to it.

And to tell you the truth, I did stop digging there. On my own land!

Three Acadians on the Ice

told by Hyacinthe Chiasson, one of the three men

(English begins on page 41)

En 1874, le 27 Janvier, nous partions le matin vers six heures de chez nous, Placide Boudreau et moi. Nous étions parti pour aller prendre les glaces a la pointe du Ouest de L'ile de Chéticamp. La nous avons rencontré Hypolite LeFort qui partait lui aussi pour aller faire sa tournee sur les glaces. Il était très content de nous rencontrer pour aller de compagnie avec nous. Alors nous partîmes et nous avons prit les glaces vers sept heures du matin. Dans ce temps-la nous prenions l'habitude de nos ancêtres, nous avions seulement qu'un baton et une garcette pour sauvetage.

Nous nous mimes en marche, le temps était favorable, les glaces étaient solides, nous marchions sans appréhensions. De la, nous avons marché sans relache a peu près six milles droit au large. Alors nous nous sommes arrêté pour manger une bouchée. La temperature était toujours belle et nous prétendions avoir le temps de revenir de jour a la terre ferme. Jusqu'alors nous n'avions pas eu de succès, nous n'avions pu voir un seul loup marin. Comme on avait pas l'habitude de

27

porter des montres dans ses poches, on pensait qu'il était a peu près une heure de l'apres-midi. Alors nous partimes a revenir sur notre chemin. Chemin faisant, nous nous appercûmes que les glaces commencaient a bouger. Comme la température était favorable et que le vent était toujours du Nord-Ouest, on s'en effrayait pas. La marche continue plus vite, on marchait sans relache a revenir sur nos pas.

Quand arrivé a l'ouverture de la glace, nous fûmes surprit car nous ne pensions pas rencontrer d'ouverture du tout, le froid étant un peu intense a cette saison de l'année, le frimat nous faisait paraitre l'eau de la couleur des glaces. Ce fut le moment le plus terrible a l'arrivée au bord de l'eau sans l'avoir apper-cu d'avance. La distance de l'ouverture était asser large que nous ne pouvions pas juger la distance de la largeur de l'eau qui nous faisait face.

Alors nous nous sommes decidé de courir sur l'est a filer sur le bord de l'ouverture. Nous fimes a peu près un mille a courir a toute jambe mais nous étions fatigués et nous fûmes obligé d'arrêter. Nous ne voyions pas lieu de pouvoir trouver un passage a l'est et nous decidames de revenir sur notre chemin en pensant que nous allions nous arreté ou nous avions accosté a l'ouverture en revenant du large. Nous pensions que si nos familles se mettaient inquiet de nous autres, qu'elles pourraient venir a notre aide en canot pour nous traverser l'ouverture de l'eau.

Comme il était un peu tard, nous primes un repos en attendant si personne ne viendrait a notre secours. Comme d'habitude, on avait pas la coutume de porter beaucoup de provisions a manger, pensant qu'on serait revenu le même jour pour souper avec nos familles. Comme nous avions deja prit un petit repas le midi, il nous restait pas grandes choses a manger dans nos poches, et le soir nous mangions tout ce qui restait. Il était a peu pres huit heures du soir et nous pensions qu'on était environ deux milles de la terre ferme.

Comme nous étions a observer les glaces nous aperçûmes que la bain de glace qu'il y avait près de la terre ferme était décaper et venait boucher l'ouverture de l'eau ce qui nous donnait une chance de debarquer sur les glaces qui avaient bouché l'ouverture. Alors nous avons continué notre chemin vers la terre mais quand nous sommes arrivé a l'ouverture de l'eau qui séparait le terre avec les glaces, nous jugions que nous étions environ trois quarts de mille de la terre ferme.

Avant cela la temperature était favorable et alors nous avons commencé a crier de toutes nos forces pour voir si personne ne viendrait pas a notre secours. Nous entendions l'écho de nos voix répéter dans les montagnes mais pas de réponse humaine. Nous arrêtames la a peu près un quart d'heure a attendre si quelque-uns viendraient a notre secours. Après tout le travail qu'on avait fait, on commencait a avoir faim et on aurait bien voulu être dans ses familles pour prendre un bon souper.

Comme on ne pouvait pas attendre de secours, on a décidé de faire du travail pour nous autres mêmes. On a prit a marcher sur l'est en pensant qu'on trouverait peut-être des pointes de glaces qui approcheraient la terre. Quand on arrivait a ces pointes, de temps en temps on arrêtait puis on criait pour essayer de se faire entendre mais sans succès. La nuit était obscure, point d'etoiles ni de lune, le temps était très couvert. À partir de la pointe du Ouest a la pointe de l'est (Enragée) de l'ile de Cheticamp nous avions cherché tous les moyens pour pouvoir trouver une pointe de glace qui aurait pu allonger au bordage de terre. Nous n'osions pas nous exposé trop craignant de tomber dans des mauvais trous et pas pouvoir nous sauver la vie si possible.

Arrivé a la pointe Enragée, nous arrêtames et on commencà encore a crier pour voir si il y avait pas de moyens de trouver de l'assistance. On jugeait qu'il était a peu près minuit. Comme on était a consulter quoi faire, le vent s'éleva de l'est avec une tempête de neige. Alors nous fûmes obligé de marcher un peu plus au large pour retrouver les glaces solides et nous trouvâmes une haie de glaces qui nous donnait un abri en attendant que le jour vint.

Quand le jour commenca a se faire, la tempête de neige commenca a apaiser et la température devient plus douce. Nous commencâmes a marcher vers l'est sans aucun espoir de remettre le pied sur la terre. Nous avons marché a peu pres sept milles sur l'est jusqu'au Cap Rouge, village de pêche habité par des Acadiens comme nous. Nous pensions comme c'étaient des pêcheurs, qu'on pourrait peut-être avoir du secours car ils avaient des canots. On était environ un mille et demi au large de la terre. On s'est dit les uns aux autres qu'on allait mettre des enseignes pour qu'ils puissent nous voir. Alors nous avons laissé nos gilets pour les pendre au bout de nos batons pour qu'ils puissent nous apercevoir plus facilement. Ils nous ont bien aperçût mais le vent était beaucoup fort et ils n'ont pas voulu risquer leurs vies pour les notres. Si ils avaient eu notre pensée, ils auraient seulement eu la peine d'envoyer un canot en drive. Si la pensée avait aussi bien pu servir de Téléphone, on aurait conter ce qu'il y avait a faire. Ils auraient pu mettre des rames et du pain dans le canot car la faim nous tourmentait déja. On aurait pu facilement atteindre le canot pour nous garder un sauvetage pour quand le vent aurait été calme et on aurait facilement atteint la terre.

On a attendu a peu près une demie heure pour voir si cette pensée ne leurs viendrait pas cest-a-dire ce qu'on pensait qu'ils auraient pu faire facilement. Quand nous avons vu que nous aurions pas d'assistance, nous avons prit a marcher vers l'ouest.

La température était devenue plus douce et le vent était de Sud. La température était assez douce que nous marchions dans l'eau parfois jusqu'a mi-jambes. Le vent et le courant portaient les glaces avec une si grande rapidité, que pour nous tenir en dedans du Cap Saint Laurent, nous étions obligé de marcher vers l'ouest sans relache car une fois dépassé le Cap Saint Laurent il n'y avait plus de sauvetage. Comme on était avec rien a manger, on sentait que le courage et la force commencaient a diminuer. On marchait toujours vers l'ouest. Vers le midi, M. Placide Boudreau qui était le plus jeune des trois a commencé a manquer de force. Alors j'ai dis a Hypolite LeFort: "Que ferait-on de notre ami si ses forces viennent a lui manquer?" Hypolite m'a repondu: "Chacun pour soi." "Il vaut mieux le laisser là que de rester avec lui quand nous pourrons travailler a gagner la terre."

Tout ce temps, nous n'avions rien a manger et nos forces diminuaient de plus en plus. Nous cherchions dans notre marche pour un loup marin ou autre chose qu'on aurait pu manger mais inutile. Cela nous a forcé a prendre nos couteaux et a lever l'écorce de nos batons. Comme ils étaient de bois franc, on les prenait pour nourriture. Les batons étaient lourds assez mais on aurait aimé qu'ils auraient été encore plus lourds cest-a-dire qu'on aurait eu encore plus d'écorce a manger. Ceci était sur le deuxieme jour vers midi. Le reste du voyage s'est terminé avec de la glace seulement pour toute nourriture. Vous pouvez voir par ce recit de la nourriture que nous prenions que l'on était pas aux noces.

Nous avons parlé il y a quelques instants que les forces commencaient a manquer a Placide Boudreau. Toutefois il nous a suivi jusqu'a quatre heures de l'apres-midi alors que nous avons été arrêtés par une ouverture qui faisait le Nord Ouest. Nous avons alors été obliges de nous campér pour la nuit. On etait arrêté de marcher vers l'ouest et le vent et le courant poussaient toujours les glaces vers l'est a notre désavantage. On vous a parlé du Cap Rouge. A cette heure-la, vers quatre heures, on a examiné la distance qu'on avait fait vers l'est malgre avoir marche toute la journee vers l'ouest. L'on jugeait que les maisons du Cap Rouge se trouvaient a une distance de sept ou huit milles au Sud.

Alors nous cherchâmes un refuge pour la nuit. Nous avons examiner tout autour de nous et nous avons trouvé un endroit favorable pour la nuit quoique ce n'était pas un lit de plumes mais c'était le meilleur que nous pouvions trouver. Notre lit de plumes pour la nuit était a l'abri d'une haie de glaces ou le fond de la glace etait passablement uni. Pour couverture nous avions un autre glacon avec un espace en dessous de trois a quatre pieds en carré. Cela aurait pu couché trois hommes mais nous avions change notre dessein. Nous couchions deux sur la glace et le troisieme pardessus les deux autres afin de pouvoir nous tenir chaudles uns contre les autres.

Comme vous le savez, la journée avait été belle, les glaces étaient beaucoup humides et cela prenait peu de temps pour l'humidité a traverser les hardes. Quand l'humidité traversait les vêtéments de celui qui était dessous, on changeait de

places. On fit cela jusqu'a minuit afin de nous tenir chaud. Comme nous étions tous trempés des
pieds aux genoux et que nos souliers étaient
troués par la marche dans l'eau et la neige fondue,
nous étions obligé de marcher de temps en temps
pour nous protéger contre le froid. Nous nous
sommes levé, Hypolite LeFort et moi. Ce n'était
pas que nous avions bien dormi, au contraire nous
n'avions pas pu fermer l'oeuil. Placide Boudreau,
étant beaucoup fatigué de la veille, dormait
comme si il eut été sur un sofa.

On s'est mit a marcher M. LeFort et moi
alentour, allant et venant, de l'endroit que nous
avions preparé la veille pour nous coucher. Tout en
marchant j'ai dis a M. LeFort: "Ecoute avec moi. Il
me semble que j'entends sonner une cloche." M.
LeFort m'a repondu qu'il croyait qu'il avait entendu un son de cloche lui aussi. Alors j'ai dis a M. Le-
Fort: "Comme la cloche de notre église a été bénite
pour toute chose, il se pourrait qu'ils l'auraient
sonné pour nous donner du courage peut-etre."
Touc ce temps-la, M. Boudreau dormait. En faisant notre marche, nous nous apper-cûmes que la
glace qui faisait notre trottoir commencait a raffer-
mir. Alors j'ai dis a M. LeFort: "Il faut aller réveill-
er M. Boudreau car il fait froid et il va se laisser
geler a la glace et peut-être qu'il y mourra." Alors
nous avons été réveillé M. Boudreau qui dormait et
une fois réveillé, il se sentait avec plus de courage.
Nous avons reprit notre marche ordinaire sur la
glace en attendant le jour.

Au jour, le vent était change au Nord Ouest et il faisait froid. Nous marchions vers la terre. On allait aussi vite qu'on pouvait. On courrait des fois, et en allant, on éxaminait tout le long de la route pour voir si l'on pouvait pas tuer un loup marin ou quelque sorte d'oiseau car la faim s'enparait de nous. Malheureusement on ne put trouver aucune sorte de nourriture et on fut obligé de continuer notre toute sans manger. C'était une journée froide mais le temps n'était pas nuageux. Les montagnes nous paraissaient assez loin que nous pensions jamais pouvoir y arriver.

Nous avons marché de l'aurore jusqu'a onze heures et demie du matin et alors nous avons éxaminer pour un passage a la terre car nous n'étions plus qu'a cinquante brasses du rivage. Nous avons regardé tout autour pour voir ou il y aurait une chance a débarquer, a l'est et a l'ouest mais c'était égal partout. Apres avoir consulté entre nous ce que nous allions faire, je leur ai dit: "C'est moi qui a guider l'affaire dupuis que nous sommes parti, et c'est encore moi qui vas etre obligé de faire ce passage le premier a la terre ferme." Car la distance n'était que trente verges et la glace n'était pas bien solide, ce n'était seulement que des morceaux de glaces et du foulange.

Il était impossible de marcher mais il fallait se trainer a plat ventre pour arriver au rivage. Alors nous avons nouées nos trois garcettes bout a bout et j'ai prit le bout et je me l'ai amarré autour du corps en leurs disant que s'ils voyaient que je passait au travers de cette glace et que j'allait au fond, de me retirer du trou et de me ramener avec eux sur la glace. J'ai traverser de cette manière et quand j'ai été au bout de la corde, je n'était plus qu'a trois ou quatre brasses de la côte. Alors comme je voyais que je pouvais me rendre, je leurs ai renvoyé la corde comme j'avais dessein de le faire quand je serais traversé, et je m'ai rendu heureusement sur le rivage. Les deux autres ont fait comme moi et ce sont aussi rendu aussi heureusement a la terre ferme.

Avant de descendre sur la terre, nous avions éxaminer pour voir si on pouvait réconnaitre ou on était. Il y avait une grande vallé se trouvant a l'est de nous et nous pensions que c'était Fishing Cove, un village d'Ecossais pour la pêche. Nous nous avons dit que si nous pouvions parvenir a cet endroit que nous serions les bienvenus, car ils connaissaient les gens de Cheticamp. Alors nous avons monté le Cap dans les grosses pierres et en haut, on s'est arrête pour causer quelques minutes. Prenant la parole j'ai dit aux autres: "Le temps que nous étions sur les glaces, il me semblait que je n'avais pas perdu de force. Mais a présent que nous sommes débarrassé du travail de descendre il me semble que le pire n'est pas fait, et quoique rassuré, le courage et les forces me manquent. Mais il faut prendre courage et si c'est Fishing Cove qui est a l'est, nous n'avons pas bien loin a marcher pour nous y rendre en passant par les montagnes."

Comme c'était pres de la côte, il y avait

seulement des petits arbres d'épinette et parfois nous étions obligé de marcher de quatre pattes pour pouvoir faire du chemin. Arrivés a la vallée que nous croyons être la Fraser, nous voyions pas aucune habitations, ni monde ni maisons, pas rien du tout. Je leur ai alors dit que il ne fallait pas nous penser écarté, que par ce qu'on avait entendu dire a nos grands parents, on était pres de la rivière a Anselm. Alors comme on faisait l'est, on a continué a aller dan la même direction et avant longtemps on a arrivé a cette rivière que nos parents appelaient la rivière a Anselm.

Apres cela on a encore marcher dans la pente de la montagne en marchant sous les petits arbres et après avoir marcher pour une bonne distance on a arrivé a un désert. Dans ce désert il faisait beau a marcher et apres avoir marche quelques instants, quelle fut notre joie d'apercevoir une petite maison en avant de nous. Cela nous a donné du courage et en approchant nous avons été contents de constater qu'il sortait de la fumée de la cheminée de cette petite maison ce qui nous demontrait que la maison était habitée. Arrivé a la maison, on frappe a la porte et on vient nous ouvrir a notre grande satisfaction et on nous souhaite le bonjour.

Ils étaient effrayés de nous voir car ils savaient que nous n'étions pas du monde du voisinage. L'homme de la maison nous a demandé d'ou nous venions et on lui a repondu que nous venions de sur les glaces, qu'on était des naufragés, enfin on lui a raconte toutes nos misères. Alors j'ai dit a M. LeFort: "Tu as plus de courage que moi." "Quand même que j'aurais pu parler Anglais comme toi, je n'aurais pu repondre a toutes les questions qu'il te demandait." Le maître nous a dit que nous étions les bienvenus mais que nous avions bien mal tombé car nous étions dans une bien pauvre maison. Pour toute nourriture ils avaient du hareng et des patates et pour breuvage de l'avoine routi trempée. Il nous ont fait cuire du hareng et des patates et nous ont avont mangé.

Il y avait trois fois vingt-quatre heures qu'on avait seulement l'ecorce de nos batons et des morceaux de glaces pour nourriture. On simaginait que c'était de la nourriture mais c'était loin d'en être une, au contraire. Quand le hareng et les patates ont été cuits, on s'est mit a table pour prendre le repas si longtemps attendu mais on avait la bouche si pleine de fièvre occasionné par être si longtemps sans manger que nous trouvions aucun bon gout a la nourriture qui nous était donné. On a pas manger plus qu'a l'ordinaire pour la première fois car après ce long jeûne on avait peur de se rendre malade.

Le repas fini, comme il n'y avait pas de poêle, seulement qu'une grande cheminée, on a été cherché un peu de paille a la grange et l'ayant étendue en avant de la cheminée, on s'est couché dessus et on a prit un bon repos sur cette couchette de paille qui nous avait ete preparé. A l'heure du souper, on nous a reveillé et on nous a preparé un même repas comme le premier. Le souper fini, la couchette de paille se prépare cette fois-ci pour toute la famille.

Le lendemain matin on se lève vers les sept heures très bien reposés. Apres avoir déjeuné, vers huit heures on quitte la petite maison en les remerciant beaucoup de l'hospitalité qu'ils nous avaient donné. On ne pouvait en faire plus car on avait pas d'argent dans nos poches pour les récompenser de ce qu'ils avaient fait pour nous. On leurs a dit bien sincèrement que si quelquefois ils venaient a Cheticamp, cest-a-dire au Havre de L'est, de s'informer pour nous et qu'on ferait son possible pour témpigner notre reconnaissance.

On avait pas de Téléphone ni Télégraph alors pour laisser savoir a nos parents de notre sauvetage et ils nous croyaient bien perdus. Ainsi nous avons été obligé de prendre notre route vers l'est, vers Aspy Bay pour prendre notre route revenir a notre foyer paternel. On a marcher a peu près un mille et nous étions au Cap Saint Laurent. Arrivé la, nous avons considéré le langer que nous avions couru. Si nous avions dépasse le Cap Saint Laurent sur les glaces, il n'y avait aucun espoir de sauvetage car les glaces une fois dépassée le Cap, se dispersent, un morceau ici et un morceau là et il n'y a plus de terre pour les arrêter.

Supplement by Paul V. Boudreau, brother of Placide Boudreau: En mettant les pieds a terre, la premiere chose fut de jeter les batons au large avec

39

promesse de ne plus jamais retourner sur les glaces. Ils dormirent jusqu'au lendemain et Polite LeFort qui avait gele les pieds fut oblige de prendre un guide avec un cheval pour le remener au Cap Rouge. La Michel McKinnon vint avertir a Petit Etang et Eucisse Chiasson arriva chez mon pere, Venant Boudreau a onze heures en nuit avertir les parents qu'ils étaient sauvez. Toute la famille se leva pour faire la priere car mon pere, Venant Boudreau, était le pere de Placide Boudreau, un des descape.

Le Pere Giroir, Cure de la Paroisse, qui avais toujours prier Saint Joseph durant leurs naufrage, fut aussi averti, et quand il su la nouvelle, sortant du lit, il leva les bras au Ciel en criant: "Bon Saint Joseph! Vous m'avez exaucer."

Three Acadians on the Ice

re-told by Rosie Aucoin Grace

On January 27th, 1874, myself and Placide Boudreau left around six o'clock in the morning. We
were going seal hunting on the ice off the western
point of Cheticamp Island. Along the way, we met
up with Hypolite LeFort who was also going hunting on the ice. He was very pleased to join up with
us. We got on the ice around seven o'clock in the
morning. In those days, we did as our ancestors,
we only carried a wooden stick and a rope for
protection.

We started to walk. The weather was good,
the ice was solid, we walked without apprehen-
sion. We walked without stopping for about six
miles towards the open sea. We took a break and
had a bite to eat. The weather was holding up and
we anticipated returning the same day to firm
ground. Up until then, we'd had no success in
spotting any seals. As we didn't have the habit of
wearing any watches in our pockets, we guessed
that it was about one o'clock in the afternoon. We
decided to backtrack towards home. As we walked,
we noticed that the ice was starting to move. As
the weather was favourable and the wind was always from the northwest, we were not worried.
We walked a faster pace without stopping.

We were quite surprised when we suddenly arrived at an opening in the ice, a stretch of water. It was a terrible moment as this was unexpected during such a cold season. The mist from the cold made the water look the same colour as that of the ice; therefore it was deceiving from a distance. The opening was so large, we couldn't judge the distance of water we had to face.

We decided to run along the edge of the opening towards the east. We ran as fast as we could for about a mile but we soon got tired and had to stop. We couldn't find any passage in the eastern direction so we decided to return to where we had first found the opening. We figured that if our families began to get worried about us, they could come to our rescue by way of canoe (*canot* in the French).

It was getting late and we decided to rest for a while, waiting to see if someone would come for us. As usual, we hadn't brought much food along as we had expected to be home with our families by supper time. We had already eaten a meal that day so we had very little food left, the remainder served as the meal that night. It was about eight o'clock in the evening and we figured that we were approximately two miles from solid ground.

As we observed the ice, we noticed that ice near the solid ground was unattached and coming towards us, blocking the opening. This gave us a chance to embark on the ice that was blocking the opening. We continued our walk towards solid ground but when we arrived at the water between the ground and the opening, we judged that we were still approximately three quarters of a mile from solid ground.

Up until now, the weather was favourable so we decided to try screaming for help. We shouted with all our might to see if anyone would come to our rescue. We could hear our voices echo in the mountains but no human response. We waited for about fifteen minutes to see if someone would hear us. After all this work, we began to get hungry and wished we were home with our families for a good supper.

As we couldn't just wait there for someone to rescue us, we had to take matters into our own hands. We started walking in the eastern direction towards blocks of ice that might bring us closer to solid ground. From time to time, whenever we arrived on such ice, we'd shout out in cries for help but with no success. The night was very dark, no moon or stars in sight, the sky was very cloudy. From the western point to the eastern point of Cheticamp Island (La Pointe Enragée where the Cheticamp lighthouse is today), we searched for ways of finding blocks of ice that would stretch out towards solid ground. We hesitated to expose ourselves too much as there was danger of falling into holes and risking our lives.

When we arrived at "La Pointe Enragée," we continued our cries for help in hopes that someone would come to our assistance. We estimated that it was around midnight. As we discussed our situation, the wind picked up from the east followed by a snow storm. We were therefore forced to walk towards open sea to find solid ice. We found a pile of ice that provided some shelter for us until daybreak.

At the crack of dawn, the snow storm started to subside and the temperature was getting milder. We started walking again towards the east without much hope of ever setting foot on solid ground again. We walked for about seven miles east until we arrived near Cap Rouge, a small fishing village inhabited by Acadians like us. We thought since they were fishermen who had canoes, we might be rescued. We were approximately one mile and a half from the coast. To make ourselves more visible so that someone might spot us, we hung our jackets on the end of our wooden sticks to use as a signal. Someone did notice us but the wind was strong and they didn't want to risk their lives trying to save us. If they could have read our thoughts, they would have simply sent us a canoe. If they could have reached us by telephone, we could have told them what to do. They could have put oars and bread in a canoe as by then our hunger was tormenting us. We could have simply kept the canoe as our aid for rescue and waited until the wind calmed down, then easily have reached solid ground.

We waited for about one half hour to see if someone might think of this form of rescue as we thought it could easily be done. When we realized that we wouldn't be receiving any assistance, we started walking towards the west.

The temperature was milder and the wind was now from the south. The temperature was so mild that at times we walked in water up to our knees. The wind and current carried the ice in such rapidness that in order to stay within Cape St. Lawrence we had to walk fast towards the west, as once past Cape St. Lawrence, there would be no rescue....

Hungry and tired, our strength and courage started to diminish. We continued to walk towards the west. Placide Boudreau who was the youngest of the three, started to get really weak. I said to Hypolite LeFort: "What will happen if our friend loses all his strength?" Hypolite responded with: "Everyone for themselves. It's better to leave him here to rest while we continue to try to gain solid ground."

All this time and still we had nothing to eat, we were getting weaker. We searched for seals or anything else that we could eat but it was useless. We had no other option but to use our knives and carve the bark from our wooden sticks to use as nourishment. The sticks were heavy as it was but we would have wanted them even bigger so more bark would have been available. This was on the second day around noon. We only had ice as nourishment for the rest of the journey. You can see by what we had to eat, it certainly wasn't a feast!

As we mentioned earlier, Placide Boudreau was getting weaker. He followed us until four o'clock in the afternoon when we arrived at an opening facing northwest. We were then obligated to camp for the night. We had stopped walking towards the west and the wind and current was forever pushing the ice towards the east to our disadvantage. I spoke earlier of Cap Rouge. At this hour, four o'clock, we examined the distance that we had gained towards the east although we had walked all day towards the west. We estimated the houses at Cap Rouge were at a distance of about seven or eight miles south.

We then searched for shelter for the night. We looked all around us and finally although it wasn't a feather bed, we did manage to find a bit of shelter. It was the best we could do. Our feather bed for the night was a pile of ice where the bottom was level and somewhat smooth. For cover there was a piece of ice hanging over us about three to four feet square. It was big enough for three people but we decided to sleep two on the ice with one of us on top in order to keep more warm.

As you know, the temperature was milder causing the ice to be wet and humid, taking no time at all to get our clothes soaked. When the humidity got too bad for the person underneath, we'd trade places. We did this until midnight in order to keep warm. As we were wet from our feet to our knees and our shoes were full of holes from all that walking in the water and slush, we were forced to keep active and walk to protect us from the cold. Hypolite and I got up first. It wasn't that we had received a good night's sleep but to the contrary, never slept a wink. Placide Boudreau, so fatigued from the night before, slept as if he was on a sofa.

We started to pace back and forth, myself and Hypolite LeFort. While pacing I said to Hypolite LeFort: "I think I hear the sound of a bell ringing." Hypolite answered that he thought he heard it too. I then said to Hypolite: "As the bell from our church has been blessed for everything, it's possible that it's being rung to give us courage." All this time, Placide Boudreau was sleeping. While pacing, we noticed that the ice was getting firmer. I said to Hypolite: "We have to wake up Placide Boudreau, as the ice is getting colder and he'll freeze against the ice, maybe even die." We therefore woke up Placide. Once he was awake, he felt stronger, better. We resumed our walk on the ice waiting for daybreak.

As a new day began, the wind had shifted from the northwest and it was very cold. We walked towards solid ground. We were going as fast as we could. At times we even ran, always looking out for seals or birds that we could kill to eat as pangs of hunger often took over. Unfortunately we found nothing and had to continue our journey without nourishment. It was a very cold day but not cloudy. The mountains looked so far away that we thought we'd never get to them.

We walked from dawn until eleven thirty in the morning. When we examined the passage to solid ground, we were about fifty fathoms from the coast. We looked towards the east and the west to see if there was a place that we could disembark but it was the same everywhere. After consultation among us I said: "I've been guiding us through all this since we started and I'll have to be the first one to make the passage to solid ground." The distance was but thirty yards and the ice wasn't very solid—thirty yards of floes covered with snow that floated around here and there.

It was impossible to walk so we had to crawl on our stomachs. I tied our ropes around my mid-section and started to cross with the understanding that if I went underneath the water, they should bring me back up. When I arrived at the end of the ropes, I was but three to four fathoms from the coast. I knew I could make it so I sent the rope back to the others. We fortunately all made it to the solid ground in this manner.

Before setting off on foot again, we had to try to recognize where we were. To the west of us was a valley that we thought could be Fishing Cove, a small Scottish village used for fishing. We told ourselves that if we could make it to the village we would be welcome as they knew some people from Cheticamp. Therefore we continued and climbed the huge boulders and once on top we stopped for a few minutes to talk. I said: "While we were on the ice, it seems I never got that weak but now that the worst of the work is over, I feel that my courage and strength is going. Guess we have to keep our courage up and if that's Fishing Cove to the east of us, we don't have far to walk by way of the mountain."

As we were close to the coast, we had to walk through small pine trees and at times even crawl to make our way. Once we arrived at a valley that we thought could be La Fraser (river), we saw no habitation, no people, no houses, nothing at all. I told them not to think that we were lost because we'd often heard our grandparents explain a place similar to this called "La Rivière à Anselm." Therefore we continued in the same western direction, soon to arrive at the Rivière à Anselm as described by our grandparents.

We then walked downhill on the mountain, walking underneath pine trees and after quite some distance arrived at a clearing (or meadow). It was nice walking through the clearing and after a few moments, we noticed a small house before us. This gave us courage and we were happy to see smoke rising from the chimney, indicating that the house was occupied. We arrived at the house, knocked at the door and were warmly greeted.

They were astonished to see us, strangers in their surroundings. The man of the house asked us where we were from. We explained the whole story of being lost on the ice and the misery we went through. I said to Hypolite LeFort: "You have more courage than me. Even if I could speak English like you, I couldn't have anwered all the questions he asked." The master of the house told us we were welcome in his home but unfortunately they were very poor. All they had to eat was herring, potatoes and for beverage, soaked roasted oats.

They cooked us a meal. It had been three times twenty-four hours in which all we had to eat was the bark from our wooden sticks and ice. We had imagined at the time that it was food but it was far from it. We sat down at the table for a meal discovering that we had difficulty eating. We found no taste in the food, suffering from sores in our mouths and such a long period of time without food. We didn't eat more than ordinarily as we were scared to get sick from all the fasting we'd had to do.

After the meal, since there was no stove, we went to get some straw in the barn and made a few straw beds by the chimney. At supper time, we were awakened and served the same meal as before. The straw beds were then laid out for the entire family.

The next morning, well rested, we got up around seven o'clock. After breakfast, at eight o'clock, we left the small house, thanking them for their hospitality. We could only thank them as we had no money in our pockets to repay them for what they'd done for us. We told them sincerely that if they should ever be in Cheticamp, that is Eastern Harbour, they should look us up and we'd do our best to show our gratitude.

We had no telephone or telegraph to let our families know that we were safe and they thought we were lost never to return. We had to take the eastern direction, towards Aspy Bay so that we could return to our homes. We walked for about a mile and arrived at Cape St. Lawrence. Once there, we considered what an ordeal we'd been through. It was a close call because if we had passed Cape St. Lawrence, there would have been no hope for rescue as the ice breaks up in pieces and there's no solid ground to stop it.

Supplement by Paul V. Boudreau, brother of Placide Boudreau: When they finally had their feet on solid ground, the first thing they did was take their wooden sticks and throw them out to sea with a promise never to return to the ice. They slept until the next morning and Polite LeFort that had both feet frozen had to be taken by a guide on horse to Cap Rouge.

Michel McKinnon came to Petit Etang with the news that they were safe and Eucisse Chiasson came to my father's home, Venant Boudreau, at eleven o'clock at night to inform my parents that they were safe. The whole family got up to pray as my father, Venant Boudreau, was the father of Placide Boudreau, one of the lost men.

Father Giroir, the parish priest, who had always prayed to Saint Joseph during the ordeal, was told of their return and when he received the news, he got up, lifted his arms to the sky while shouting: "Good Saint Joseph, you have listened and answered my prayers!"

Madame Elizabeth Muise—Placide Boudreau's niece—gave us the manuscript for "Three Acadians on the Ice" in French; Ulysses LeLievre first told us about this remarkable tale.

Horses in the Coal Mine

told by Archie MacDonald

I'll tell you a story about the horses.

The horses in Florence Colliery one time, and in most of the collieries, were badly used. Now it wasn't that they were poorly fed or anything, but they were overworked. A good horse, she'd work on the day shift. And the drivers were a contrary crowd, a lot of them, and they pretty well ran the pit. You couldn't get along without them. If they had dug in their heels about something, well, they wouldn't go down; they'd stay on the surface and the pit would be idle.

So they were having a problem with the horses. The good horses were overworked and the bad horses would be standing in.

So the underground manager, he had a half-brother that was quite a tough character, but he loved horses, very fond of horses. He was what you might call in those days a barroom fighter—big, heavy, stocky fellow, as tall as you are, and heavier. Loved horses, and he hated the drivers. And I bet you the underground manager, his half-brother, appointed him as the road boss especially in charge of horses.

And he wandered around the stables and looked over all the horses. A horse that came in, the driver'd come with him, the way the law said—the contract said he had to take his horse in and secure him in the stable. He just didn't turn him loose, let him go in the stable. The horse would sense when he was getting handy the stable, and he'd start hurrying up, and the driver'd have to go along, take him in under control, and take his bridle off and the bit that was in his mouth, and the heavy leather piece over his head, where if he bumped his head he wouldn't knock his scalp off. It was a "cap" they called it.

In the afternoon and evening, when the horses would be coming in, this big husky fellow would watch them coming in, looking for any bruises or scrapes or anything like that. And if he did, he'd hold them up—"Just a minute, I want to have a look at that"—and he'd hold them up—"How did this happen?" And the driver had to have a good reason for it, or the first thing he knew, the fellow'd have him by the throat and want to know how it happened. And he had to tell him. And there were none of the drivers tough enough to back this fellow up.

And I bet you in three months, three months or less, the horses were in spic-and-span condition, no scrapes or bruises or anything like that, because they were afraid of this fellow. And they had good reason to be afraid of him, because when this fellow came, he said he hated drivers, especially a driver that was hard on his horse. That fellow, he had no quarter for them at all. He'd get him off that horse, or he had to start treating his horses better, or the other fellow'd go and beat him up. He'd do it. There'd be nobody around, and he'd get him in a corner of the stable and rough him up. So he knew he was up against his master then, the man that was looking after the horses. If he was taking a horse out, he was going to take it back in good shape. And it was a true story.

That fellow lived to be an old man. He retired. But he loved horses. And he could not tolerate in any way, shape, or form a driver that abused his horse. Wouldn't put up with it. (And he re-trained the drivers?) He sure did. Nobody'd tackle a horse or damage a horse while this fellow was on.

Alex Gillis and the Big Sleigh or, "The Servant on the Mountain"

It was for firewood. It's very steep, part of that mountain. It's a continuation of Cape Mabou. Well, I suppose it'd be Mabou Mountain, Northeast. Fall of 1946.

(*Did you used to take wood off of that mountain before?*) Oh, yes. I remember one December my father and three of us, of the sons—it took us three weeks to take the winter's wood down. And I figure—I didn't have my stopwatch—but this came down in less than a minute.

It took us just a day and a half to build it, two of us. Two heavy bird's-eye maple skids, thirty feet long. And we nicked them to prevent the cables from wearing. The firewood went on full length—trees went on full length—crossways. The skids were about eleven feet apart. And three cross members. And they were nicked down and bored, drilled, and heavy drift-bolts put in, twelve of them in the cross members. Then, it had two binders on, steel wire. Binding the wood, the load.

The trees were full length across. The skids were about thirty feet long. But sideways it would be, depending on the trees—well, around forty feet

55

in width. And about three feet thick, high. You can figure out how many cords that would be.

We had to tie it to a tree—we had steel cable, old mining cable. And we tied it to anchor it, 'cause it was on the slope. And we tried to put rollers under it, to be ready to go. The ditches were in under it.

(*Let me take you back. This was a place where you usually had gotten wood, right?*) Lower down. We never took it off the top. It's better higher. We knew of one place where there's a valley, and the trees were straighter and longer. Easier to split, and so on. (*And how far up the mountain are we talking about?*) Where the sleigh was? Just at the top, where you can see—one of those bare spots there. (*And how far did you think you were going to have to travel?*) About 1200 feet, I'd say.

(*What was the old way of doing it, for you, before you built the big sleigh?*) Oh, twitching—cutting, and leaving two branches. And putting a half-hitch with a small, slim chain or a heavy rope, like we used for pitching hay in the barn. Put a couple of half-hitches on there. Sometimes you could take a few small trees. And someone'd be twitching it home with perhaps two horses. That is, when we took it off the front of the mountain. Which was quite a few hundred feet below where the sleigh was set. One horse, one time, (my brother) Angus was coming down—I was quite young then—he had one hand on the bit of the bridle, and on the hame. And the log caught—a stump, or roots of a tree. And something broke. And the horse went heels over head. It's that steep.

(*How long would it take you to get your winter's wood, before the year of the big sleigh, with all of you working?*) Three weeks, I think it took the four of us, when we took it off the front. But there's another route around—it's close to three miles, over the highway and up back. Which is up a more gradual slope with our sleighs. In the wintertime, when the snow was quite heavy.

(*So where did you get the idea to try a new method?*) Well—friction and gravity. Coasting with a little sleigh when we were young, I suppose. Something between all of that. I did house-moving, too, and different things like that. Rough construction.

(*Did you tell your father the idea? Did he think it was a good idea or not?*) Except that people were telling him that it was aimed pretty well at the barn! He didn't seem to worry. There's a deep gully running this way. The *Queen Mary* couldn't come over that, it's so steep. But people passing on the road thought it was aiming pretty well on the barn.

So we had it aimed for a brook where there was mud. We didn't care if we had to shovel mud and snow, where it would land, as long as we didn't have to climb the mountain.

(*Did you build the sleigh up at the top? Or did you build it down here and take it up?*) Oh, no. Oh, no. They were very heavy sticks. We had to take a double team up to twitch them over. They were about eighteen inches in the small end, and thirty feet long. It's a pretty heavy hardwood stick for one horse. The skids were shaped like a runner on the front. And we nicked them—we cut in about two inches all along the skid, to protect the cables from wearing into the frozen ground.

(*The skid is going longways. You cut a groove along the bottom?*) Yeah—where it would be touching the earth. Oh, it wore the bird's-eye maple down about three inches. It made them three inches less. They were smooth. (*Coming down the hill.*) Yeah. Oh, so much weight. And all those little pebbles, stones, froze. It rained. The weather would cause them to be little points. It came down very— it gained speed at the steeper part. It had to. That friction all the time, tearing the bark and wearing the wood. Oh, I'm sure of three inches off the big part, too. You had to take all those things pretty well into consideration.

We tied the skids one by one. We took them down—we had a cable on them—till we got them on a certain slope, degree, you know. And then we stopped each one, and put the cross members on. And that kept—the one tie would hold it, back to the woods, to the tree that was anchoring it.

(*So you actually built it in the woods.*) Yes. At the top of the mountain, just in that bare spot. There's a clearing at the top. (*Then did you clear some of the snow from there to the bottom?*) No. In fact we had to wait from fall until the 4th of February, 1947—before there was enough snow in the ditches, we figured that it would slide well on it. (*Before the snow was there, you did work on the mountain to prepare for this?*) Oh yes, yes. We made the ditches with one heavy horse and reliable chain traces.

(*These ditches—are you telling me you ploughed the side of the mountain?*) Two trenches. I was sighting them and (Angus) had a packsack full of pegs, and he would drive them in. You know, like the engineers do when they go. I'd sight it and I'd wave to him, either way, that he'd drive it. We got to the top, and came down. Then we came home and got the horse and the plough, a walking plough. And we went to the top. And it's so steep, we had to go zigzag—bringing the horse up, the plough. And we started.

He was the driver. He was sitting on the plough and he could sight between the horse's legs—he could keep the plough in line with the pegs. To make the ditches straight. Otherwise, twists or bends would cause the sled maybe to jump the tracks. It's very rough. If you'd let her down without ditches she'd smash to pieces quickly on the frozen ground.

(*So when you ploughed the ditches, you ploughed down the hill.*) Right. Both times. (*Both ditches.*) We'd twitched a log that we figured was about the size of the big end of the skids, to make it smooth. It made the ditch still more straight.

(*So finally you have these two ditches. You've*

ploughed them out, you've pulled the log through them. And they're about 1200 feet long. And you did that at what season of the year?) Perhaps November. Far enough back that there was no frost.

We got the team of horses to twitch the heavy timber over, for the skids. We twitched them in a way that they wouldn't take off on us. Let them down gradual until they both were (even). First one stopped, and (we) anchored (it) to the tree. And then the second one. We likely used two cables—another rope of some type—for the second one. And we got them even. And put the cross members on. We had to cut them down and set them in the skids and bore them. It was a day and a half it took us to do that.

It was tied then—two heavy skids, thirty feet long, and the three cross members of hardwood—all was wood. (*And these skids are sitting in this ditch, ready to go.*) Yes, with rollers, wooden rollers, under it. Just blocks of wood, so it would start when we'd let it go.

(*So that's done. Do you then begin to cut your firewood?*) Yes. Yes, it was after, we cut the wood. (*Did you have power saws?*) No. Bucksaws. I guess, and a crosscut for different size trees. And we built a little cabin. We'd leave home and take our lunches. He took an oil drum up, on his back, and we used it as a stove. And it's still up there! We had a bunk in there. Usually when we'd get up there, we'd have the lunch, and do the cutting. Oh, I think the cutting was done in about four or five days. (*Did you stay overnight?*) No. It was just a shelter from the snow. Just the fun of building it.

(*After four or five days your wood is cut, your sleigh is waiting, then what did you do?*) My brother twitched it over. He was in better shape to go back and forth kind of fast like that than I was. Then we rolled it on. We had timber that would raise it the height of the sleigh, the back of the sleigh. We rolled them on. We had a stopper at the front, in case they'd go too far: a pair of braces.

(Once loaded,) the binders were put on—cables lashed around the front of the skids, and back. And then put a long slim pole, hardwood pole, that would bend well. As the sleigh would travel, she'd settle. The logs would get closer together. And the extra spring in the pole was still holding it bound. A long binder does that better. We were short of steel cable. It took so many half-hitches on the cable going back to the tree, we had to use some hemp rope or manila, close to two inches in size—that we doubled it. But when she got in the frozen ditch, it just cut that right off quick, and one binder—she ran on one binder then. Which was a good thing.

We put windfalls on the front. They were good wood, too—dry—dead hardwood. We put quite a few on the front. And they started dropping off on one side, and going in under her. And they were clipping—her weight didn't raise her out—she was breaking them off—different sized sticks. Aged wood, you know. Dead wood. They were rolling in under her. And still it didn't put her off, out of the ditches—she was so heavy. And the skids were so long.

(*Had you intended for this wood to fall off and do that?*) No. One of the things that happened in her favour. (After the run) they took a sleigh-and-a-half load down off the face of the mountain. My two brothers took it home. (*This was a sleigh-and-a-half load that had fallen off?*) Yes.

(*How many normal sleigh loads do you think you had on that one big sleigh?*) About between twenty-five and thirty. (*Any idea how much something like that would weigh?*) No. I don't know the weight of hardwood. (*Would it be a winter's wood?*) Oh, yes. Over a year's wood. Of course we used— in the summertime we used fence poles and spruce kindling. They're not so hot in a house. But they used the split wood, too, for cooking meals in the old-fashioned stove. (*So that was all aboard too. That was all on this big sleigh.*) Yes. And I sawed some logs (for) the mill, too. (*All on this sleigh—some sawlogs, your winter's wood, some wood that you might use for fencing.*) I mentioned the fencing because in the summertime we used spruce for quick fires. But the hardwood is mostly for heat, heating the homes. No furnaces.

(*So tell me about the day you brought the wood down.*) Oh, we waited for a—there might have been enough snow, but we wanted the ditches full of snow, so it would crush down and form a—the weight would cause it to slide, like on ice.

That type of a day—weather came, with the snow, and the ditches seemed to be full—and we started up. When we got up there, it was snowing and raining for all those months, and it collected under. And it was solid in ice—the two skids in blue, solid ice—shaded from the sun, with the load. No bulldozer, no dynamite. We couldn't go near the sides or the front of it—too dangerous. You never knew when it might—you might just rattle something or touch something that would cause it to go. So we didn't dare go near the front or the sides of it at any time. We had to do all the work from behind.

We got a ratchet jack, a heavy ratchet jack. We took it apart and put it in two sacks, two bags, and we walked up with it. Put it together. And we jacked one skid after the other. We jacked the first one up, at the rear. And we put a little crimp or roller. And we let it down on that. And then the second one—we raised it, and we put a prop about three feet long under the rear, where we jacked it up. That was a kind of a trap ready to snap it, just be snapped. A pointed prop.

And I told him, "Try and knock it down." It was leaning, leaning, and it just—last blow did it.

She just rattled for awhile, the whole sleigh. It bounced down, and it rattled, and it cleared itself free of the ice. And she started in the nice ice trenches. The other (skid) was on a roller, and she just took off. It rattled for a little while—oh, a split second. And then she started moving.

She left us on the hill with nothing but the tools!

And the cable we had tied back. I think that one went also with it. We (had) coiled it up and threw it. We had to be careful that there was no cable would—while we would be working or watching the sleigh—that something would catch you and take you along with it. You have to be pretty careful. And the ground was frozen at that time, and quite slippery. Well, the 4th of February. It was the day after the Mabou Asylum burned down. I didn't know. But I remembered that. And I asked the keeper years after what day it was. The building burned down on the 3rd of February, 1947. And the sleigh came down on the 4th. Late in the evening. It took us quite awhile because of the jacking, the delay, because it was frozen.

(*What did it sound like when it started out?*) Oh, the crust of the earth, of the mountain, was frozen. And it made quite a roar—to us, anyway. And it disappeared for awhile. There's a dip in the face of the mountain. We couldn't see it, but we could hear the roar, so we knew it was travelling. And we could see the boulders. It was taking boulders out of the frozen ground. The weight, you know, so many of those hardwood sticks. And they were rolling—perhaps eight or ten of them— rolling, and some of them going past it. Landing on top of it—they'd stop. And the rest were rolling higher than the sleigh, over.

(*And what did it sound like when it reached*

64

the end of the road?) No sound—we didn't hear. When it left the ditches, it had nothing—like a railroad, like rails—to hold it together then. It split open. The timber that was coming out in the front—it raised one end of the cross member up. And then the blocks were rolling in under, and it took the centre one up. It raised. So she was riding with only the rear cross member. 'Cause it had hitches of the cable, of the binders, around it, together with the bolts.

It split open. The two skids went about seventy feet apart, they ended up. And she dumped the whole thing on level ground. Three things happened—the ice, freezing of the ice, and the blocks that went in under it and removed the two cross members—made it in a way that it opened out and dumped the whole load off first. It scattered about 150 feet around. We could see that, as it was scattering, before they stopped rolling. We could see them scattering.

We came down, just walked past it. They were far apart enough to chunk them up short, for to put on an ordinary sleigh, a small sleigh.

I came home and I went to bed. And my two younger brothers took it home. I think in two days. The distance wouldn't be—about a quarter of a mile. They had two horses....

People were watching from all around. We told someone that travelled—for Raleigh's or something—some people over here, neighbours, were interested—they wanted to see it come down.

Afar off, they could see it—you can see that part of the mountain. I sent a word with this fellow. There was a telephone in the house, and I think they made it known to others that wanted to see it—across the harbour.

(*So it worked well.*) Very, very well. We were pleased. I took logs down after, twitched them down. But I never made (a big sleigh) any more. They started using coal. And then the oil. (*You never made another sleigh like that?*) No. If I did, I'd have a movie camera.

My uncles on my mother's side—Mac-Phees—they built one one time—that made it worse for us. They built one of spruce booms, I think it was. And they let it down wild, without ditches. And one side of it caught the bare frozen ground and it swung it, and it aimed for the buildings. And it took a wire fence—I can only remember—the wire fence was twisted all to pieces, posts and all. But it was aiming towards the house and, perhaps, the barn. I'm not sure which would get it, the house or the barn. It swung from the direction they aimed it, about—oh, a few hundred feet away. It caught one side and it changed the course.

(*That was years before you tried it.*) Oh, yes. Years before. There was no ditch—that was my idea of making the ditches, to control it.

(*Did you ever worry about doing this? The night before, or the week before, did you have any bad dreams?*) Oh, I think the prayer covered that. I didn't worry about the barn at all. If it would

66

leave. One time my brother, younger than I, he said, "Aw, let's tear it apart. They're talking so much about it"—and hearing stories about what might happen, and what happened to the other one, over on the other hill there—not so high, but (they had) no ditches, no trenches built.

(*What did you call your sleigh? Did it have a kind of a name?*) Oh, they referred to it as "The Sleigh on the Mountain." Or, I called it "The Servant on the Mountain!"

How Johnny Murphy Tuned His Autoharp

Here's how I tune the autoharp.

I take a tune like "Home on the Range," and I play it in the Key of C. So in the centre of it—I'd call it the middle octave. Then I tune it and I go back and forth till I get all those strings in the Key of C—because you don't take in any black keys. But it takes in nearly all of what would be the white keys on the piano. You know, you don't use the sharps or flats.

And then I go to work and I take the same piece and I start to play it in the Key of F. And that takes in one black key, like a sharp, in the centre. That's one of the sharps I get.

Then I tune it back and forth from that, an octave higher and an octave lower. Then I play the same piece in the Key of G and you get two more black keys. Then I tune them the octave higher and the octave lower till I get them.

And I think you have to play the same piece in the Key of D to get that last one of those black keys. And that's how I tune the autoharp.

I never had any education in music. I don't know one note from another—but you can make a good job on tuning with that. I could tune them off of the organ or off the piano, but it doesn't sound right. But this way, you'll tune it perfect.

Johnny Murphy had a museum of musical instruments in his Northeast Margaree home.

How the Robinsons Got So Strong

told by Malcolm Blue

In the days of my youth I lived in Cape Breton Island in a large old house which my grandfather had built. My maternal grandparents lived in the valley of Kewstoke, eleven miles away by road but only six miles away across the mountain.

The Highland Scots did not make much of Christmas. It was mostly a religious reminder and was so celebrated. New Year was an entirely different matter and was well and properly celebrated.

On this occasion my father and mother took my two sisters and myself to visit our grandparents on New Year's Eve.

We journeyed across the mountain in a sleigh with two seats in it and drawn by two black horses. The mountain was very steep to climb, so my father walked behind the sleigh until we reached the top. We then rode along with bells jingling, usually at a walk until we began to descend. The horses could not be held in but rushed down the mountain at great speed until we reached our grandfather's gate.

When we got into the house we were warmly received. Our grandfather was from North Uist. Grandmother was from the Island of Rum. After a hearty dinner we sat around the stove and were entertained by stories of the past, particularly ghost stories.

When it was time to go to bed we were so scared that we could not sleep. Grandmother apparently realized this, for she came and sat on the side of the bed and told me still another story. This is it:

Do you know why the Robinsons down the road are so strong?

Long ago in Scotland, on the land farmed by John Robinson there was a hill in which the fairies lived. John had a daughter who was very beautiful. She was also an excellent cook. Her name was Jean.

John Robinson said that he did not believe in fairies and he made fun of the people who did. In any case, his sayings vexed the king of the fairies and he decided to do something about it.

One evening Jean went to call on a poor old lady. She brought her some cakes and cookies. She sat and talked until it was quite dark. She then left for home.

She did not get there, for on the way she was surrounded by the fairies and taken to the hill. The fairies were not unkind. She was given a nice clean room with a comfortable bed to sleep in.

In the morning the fairies told her that she was to bake oat bread for them. They gave her everything she needed to work with and they showed her a small bin where the meal was kept. It was as full as it could hold. They told her that

70

when she had baked all the meal in the room she could go home.

She worked hard all day and the bin was almost empty. There was some meal still on the board. Of it she made a little cake and when it was cooked she went to bed.

When she got up in the morning the bin was as full as ever. Jean baked all day long and in the evening she made another small cake of the leavings. The next morning the bin was again full. This went on for several weeks. Jean was beginning to wonder if she would ever get home.

One morning the fairies were all out except one old fairy who was toasting his toes at the fire. Suddenly he said to Jean: "I am a mortal. I was stolen from my mother when I was a baby. If you want to get home, do this. When you have the leavings on the board tonight instead of making a little cake of them, throw the leavings into the fire and the bin will be as you left it when you get up tomorrow."

That evening Jean said that she was tired and the leavings of which she used to bake a little cake she threw into the fire. When she got up in the morning the bin was exactly as she had left it. She soon baked all the meal and she then told the fairies that she was finished.

They paid her for her work and told her that they would take her home that evening after it got dark. They told her to ask for any favour that she would like to have from them. Jean gave the matter careful thought. Her father was well-to-do and the family lacked nothing. She therefore asked the fairies that all her children and their descendants would have remarkable physical strength. Her request was granted. That is why the Robinsons are so strong.

True to their promise they brought her home that night. Her father stopped saying nasty things about the fairies.

I asked Grandmother if there was any danger that they would come and take me through the night. She told me of course not, if I said my prayers. She added, "Say them with me"—and she began:

> "Ar n-Athair a tha air neamh,
> Gu naomhaichear d' ainm,
> Thigeadh do rìoghachd.
> Deanar do thoil air talamh,
> Mar a nithear air neamh...."

That was as far as I stayed awake. When I awoke day was breaking and I was hungry.

The prayer begins "Our Father...."

72

Art Langley: "Politics is Dirty"

I was mayor of Port Hawkesbury. I went on the council in 1916 first, and I think it was 1929 I was elected mayor, and then I served about sixteen years, on and off, back and forth.

And we were one of the first towns in Nova Scotia that had pavement. That was around 1928 or '30. There was no pavement in Hawkesbury.

Now Yarmouth had a mile of pavement, and Wolfville. I'm not talking about Sydney or Halifax. Antigonish didn't have it.

In the spring of the year they were getting bogged with their cars here, going back and forth—what a hell of a mess. All we were spending on this road here was about 1800 dollars a year. Well, we could get this paved for 30,000 dollars— one mile—with the best kind of pavement. Guaranteed for twenty years. Well, at 1800 dollars a year, in twenty years you've got that thing paid for. And you've got a good street.

I went to Halifax and there was a Tory government in power. Mr. Black was the Minister of Highways. And I was always a Liberal—a nasty Liberal as far as the Tories were concerned. And a Tory, Hubert Aucoin, represented this county, from Cheticamp. He and I were good friends, the very best. Now I said, "Hubert, if you can do something for me," I said, "I'll do what I can to elect

73

you." He said, "You come to Halifax and we'll see Percy Black, see what we can do for you."

I went. I said, "30,000 for one street is too much for one little town." I told Percy Black, "I understand you did something for Wolfville, you paid half of that and the same in Yarmouth. Now," I said, "do that for a Liberal."

He got up off the chair and he put his hand to his forehead like that and he walked over to the window, and he walked around and everything. "Well," he said, "I don't know how we can do it." He said to me, "You're not quiet."

So he didn't commit himself. We went away and Hubert worked on him. And at last he did it. Well, he was defeated that election then. The Liberals won that election. Poor old Hubert was defeated. I felt sorry for him—a good man, too. Well, politics—dirty, isn't it? But anyway, we got the road.

But I'll tell you how dirty the Liberals were. The road was to start down here at the harbour bridge and go north one mile up to the top of the road. And to show you how dirty they were with me, because they knew of course that I had voted for the Tories—they stopped the paving at that street over there, before it got to my home. Well, I raised hay, but that was the way it was going to be. I said, "It's not going to happen that way, my son, that is to be sure." "Well," he said, "if it doesn't, I'll fill my coat and go home." "Well, you go home," I said. "This is no place for you."

74

A representative of the Standard Pavement Company, to please me, he said, "Langley, we will finish it for nothing. When they stop there, we will finish it the rest of the way for you—but for god's sake," he said, "don't raise hell like this. It's going to affect us too."

I said, "They're not putting it over me, and I don't want to do it that way."

But they said they'd rather I let them do it. "You'll get the pavement you asked for but," he said, "quiet down and don't cross them, because it'll affect us."

And so I quieted down and Standard Pavement put that in. Politics is dirty. Oh, jeez, they're as rotten...it's amazing, terrible.

Bowden Murphy: Working for Nothing

I remember the first time I went away to work.

I worked at Goose Cove, what they call it down there, the North Shore—where that gypsum company was. I worked ten hours for one dollar. Ten cents an hour. The Quarry—I worked there. Yeah, worked there one year. That was in 1912, I think.

(*Was that the first time you left home?*) That

was the first time, yes. I think in October, if I remember right, the time I went there.

And the next time I went away from home, it was 1914, I think, or 1913. I went up to George's River, the quarry that was up there. I worked there. A dolomite quarry. It was right up on the mountain. It had to come down three chutes, 120 feet, to get to those heavy rails, a railroad. And there were three chutes. It came down a chute here, and then it went out into ton boxes. And then went down another chute. And then down the third chute, before it went down in the cars, where the train came in and picked them up. That was my second time going away.

It was all horse and cart work, then. That was down below. But up above, up on the third level where we were working, I used to run it out in the ton boxes. Sixteen cents an hour. And then they took so much off of you for the church, so much for coal. You made nothing.

We were intending to come home. My brother and I were working there at that time. We were intending to come home around Christmas, or just after Christmas. So we didn't bother laying off at Christmas, Christmas week, you see. They had a kind of clean-up week, and got everything in shape for the winter. So we stayed there.

And the two of us onto this little ton box, you know, and it wasn't inspected. See, there's an inspector there inspected every box before you used it. And when we went out with our first trip, it went down. There was a kind of a guardrail along the side, and when they tipped the box, it would strike this kind of a guardrail that was on the side of it, you see, to keep the box from going off. But there was a bolt out of the bottom, and we didn't know it. When we tipped the box, over went the whole thing, and we went behind it.

One hundred twenty feet! And it was just about that steep! (*Almost straight up and down!*) Almost up and down. And we went right to the bottom of that. There were twelve men killed in that same chute, and we're the only two that ever came out alive. (*Twelve people were killed.*) At different times, yeah. One hundred twenty feet. And when I got about halfway down, there was where the rails used to come together—one rail was above the other like this, you know, and it kind of hooked me in the back. I was about a week—I could have gone to work, but.... When I struck at the bottom—I had my sleeves rolled up to here— and when I struck at the bottom, out along that stuff that was blown up with dynamite, really sharp rock, I was skinned right up to here. But my brother, he struck right on his foot here—struck onto a piece of dolomite in the box. And he couldn't get out.

And I looked up above like this, and when you look up above 120 feet—and here was great big rocks hanging on the edge of the rails up above, over the end of the rail. And I said, "For God's sake, Raymond, if you can get out of it, boy, let's try to get out of it." And I crawled over—there was a big plank, a plank wall on each side, you know, to keep the stuff from going over. I got over there, got ahold of the top of the wall like this, in case of a rock coming down. But he couldn't get out of her.

And by and by, we saw these two fellows coming down the banks. They saw us go. They thought, of course, that was the last for us. Because we were the first ones that ever came out alive. But when I came up, I don't know—the blood was coming out of my nose, out of my mouth. Oh, I felt rotten. I heard one say, "Two people killed—brothers!" And I heard one fellow whisper to the other, he said, "That fellow must be hurt bad. The blood is coming out of his mouth and out his nose." But I heard him. I thought I was finished, oh, and what a feeling.

But anyway, they wired out to North Sydney for a doctor to come in. He came in and he said, "Where's the fellow got struck in the back with a rock?" This rock—I was going as fast as the rock was, but it caught me in the back when I hung up on this edge of the rail. I told him, I said I was probably the man—I was laying out. He checked over me, and he said, "There's no broken bones." He said, "You're lucky—no broken bones."

One week from that, I was back up in the quarry again. And all we were doing then was taking up the pipes for the winter. It was a steam drill they had. One of those pipes—they only weigh about twenty-five pounds—they wouldn't let me pick one up! But poor Raymond, my brother, he had to come home, and he was laid up for about three months.

(*Why would you do that work, instead of fish?*) Well, it was just a change, that's all. (*It wasn't for all the money you could make.*) No, no, we were making nothing.

Bill Daye: Walking Down the Deer

I know you are sick of deer hunting stories, but I must tell you this one—it is very, very strange.

One day while walking through the woods—I came up on the snowshoes as usual—I had a good long walk through the woods—I used to love to do it—I came across two deer. The snow in the woods was just about up to their knees. "Well," I said, "now I have all day to do this—I wonder can you walk a deer down? Who has the most stamina to keep it up, the deer or the man on the snowshoes?"

So I start to follow them. I followed them and followed them and followed them. I came to one place where there was another deer standing up— he was dead and frozen. Apparently his foot had been caught in something, some dead branches or something down under the snow, and he stood there and perished. Even his head was down on the snow, but he was still frozen stiff as could be.

So I kept going by him, I kept following those two deer. Sometimes I would come out on a hill—there were my two deer way far ahead of me. I would start coming, they would start galloping, going, going, going. I went from the morning to afternoon till coming on the evening.

I was just going to give it up, when I came out on the top of a hill and looked down on a field. Here were the two deer laying down. They were laying down, exhausted. They were breathing heavy, heavy, heavy. I walked down where they were. They lay there. They were looking at me, frightened, scared.

After awhile, they got up and put their two noses together. And they stood up on their hind feet and the one put his paws on the one's shoulder and the other put his paws on the other one's shoulder. And they stood up there, they put their faces together, and they laid down and paid no more attention to me. Just as much as to say, "Well, boy, here it is"—and that was some kind of a form they had to go through before they said that is the end.

So I climbed up in a great big high tree to see could I get my bearings before dark to find my way back home, maybe a shorter way than what I had come. And I took off for home. And that is the end of that story. It was very peculiar.

Hilda Mleczko and Henry's Accidents

Henry's been in lots of accidents. Yes, and it's only since he's been on pension that I've heard some of them. Pretty hair-raising thing, I'm telling you. He used to cover up from me. See, he'd go to Out-patients. Or he could have something covered up. He wouldn't tell me.

Like I remember he came home once—the only time he couldn't cover it up—he came to the door like a white-turbaned Indian. He had a great big bandage around his head. And I went as white as the bandages. "Not to worry," he said, "not to worry. It's only a scratch." That scratch was caused by a coupling link that flew off an air hose at full pressure, and Henry was hit between the eyes, right on the bridge of his nose. Now if it'd gone either way, he'd have had an eye knocked out. He was very lucky. There was no damage done to his head. He said he had hard bones.

And afterwards, he was shaving himself one day, and he was doing this and doing this. He said, "I'm going to have this dumb mark erased"— the mark from where he'd been hit. Now, all the miners, when they get cuts, when they heal, they have tattoo marks on them. Because the coal dust goes in the cuts, and it seals up—it's like a tattoo. Well, I was wondering why all the fuss, because he had had those marks all over his body, more or less. So I said, "Well, why are you worried about it, Henry?" He said, "Look." He said, "I'm branded. It's two letters—an 'I' and a 'T.'"

Well, when I looked, there it was, a complete "I" and a "T." So he said, "I'm going back and have it opened and cleaned out."

So he went back to Dr. Green. And he opened it up and cleaned it out, and Henry went happy home. But when it healed, there was the "I-T" again on his head. He said, "It's still there. I'm going back to the doctor again." Went back to Dr. Green again, and he did the same thing. Took the stitches out, and scrubbed at him real hard. And he went home. Healed again. And it was still there.

So he went back to the doctor the third time. When Dr. Green saw him walking in the door he said, "Oh, no, not you!" He said, "Henry, I've done all I can. Now," he said, "you live with it 'I-T.' And be thankful there's not an 'S-H' in front of it!" That's the truth—God's truth—that's what the man said.

So I mean, that was only a little thing. But his brother got buried under a pile of stone and coal. They wrapped the wires to stop the rake—that's the train—the rake—pit term for train. They knew that there had been a man trapped under coal, on the coal floor. And of course Henry ran, and he saw his brother's squashed lunch can and his pit cap, and he knew it was his brother. So he dug and he dug and he dug. And he held most of the weight—while they were scratching their heads and saying, "How are we going to take him out?"—he sort of burrowed underneath and took the weight of a big slab of stone that was digging into him here, and took the weight on his own back.

'Cause he said that the hardest thing he ever had to do was go and tell his sister-in-law—'cause he had to take Eddie's clothes home—the hardest thing he ever had to do was to tell his sister-in-law. Because she thought Henry was telling her that her husband was dead. But he wasn't, he was injured.... Ooo, poor man. But he was all right.

But anyway, that night when Henry came home, I put my arms around him in bed like I always did. And he moved away from me. I asked him if he was mad or something. He said, "No." I said, "Well, what's wrong?" "Well, I'll show you, but it's not very nice." He took his pyjama top off, and he showed me his back. And where the rocks had ground into him, it was like huge tiger claws all down his back, where he'd taken this weight of the rock off his brother. He's still got those scars today. But when they were fresh you could have played Oughts and Crosses (X's and O's) on them.

And then another time, he said a fellow worker got caught—his pants leg, or part of his clothing, was caught in the wheel, the wheel used for hoisting the cage to the top—the cage was the elevator that took the men from the deeps up to the top. And he got caught—it was working. And by the time they stopped it, it had ground into his leg and ground it to bits. And he's screaming, "Cut it off! Cut it off!" And by the time a workmate got the axe and severed it with one blow, it was only hanging on by a strip of flesh.

But you see—the next day they had to go to work just as if nothing had happened. They were like soldiers....

They had a rule, to say, "Don't ever get out of the rake"—the train—until it came to a full stop. Because sometimes it would get an extra surge in power. And if you happened to be standing in front of that rake, you'd go underneath the wheels, or on the side.

And Henry was with a young fellow—he hadn't been married very long. And he was in an all-fired hurry to get out of the rake. And he jumped out before it stopped, and it spurted up again. And Henry was holding onto his jacket saying, "No!" And he was left holding his jacket when he saw his mate's body go under the wheels until it was ground up like hamburger. And that's when he got all upset. He came home and he kept saying to me, "If only I didn't see him." He was walking the floor all night. "If only I didn't see him. If only I didn't see him." He never ate. But the next shift, he's down there again, walking over the same spot where it happened. He had to go to work.

Like I said, like in the war.

Strange Stories from Inverness County

John R. MacLeod: My uncle lived down here, what, about two miles. One Sunday I told Bessie, "I'm going down and see Uncle Angus." It was in the Fall, too. I walked down and was there, we were talking. A neighbor came, Joe MacDonald. And my uncle was an awful man for stories. Fearful. If he was living he'd fill a book for you.

Started talking ghost stories. I didn't mind while I was in the house. He made tea. Got dark. So I said about ten o'clock, "I must go home."

"Look," he says, "I wouldn't go up that road if you filled my dining room full of 100-dollar bills."

That was pretty bad. But MacDonald was coming halfways with me. So I was all right. But by God after I left MacDonald—I started to think to myself of all those old people that died. I got to a place down here they call the Devil's Bridge. And down in a swamp, in a dirty hole, all alders, I heard a pig. Eleven o'clock at night.

I stopped. The pig came out. Pig was as black as tar. "Well," I said, "the devil, for sure." I start to walk, the pig walked. I start to run, the pig run. I would stop, the pig would stop. Right alongside of me.

I seen the house. I said, "Okay"—it was in my mind—"Mister Devil, you'll not get to hell tonight, when I get a hold of the old 12-gauge."

85

I came in the house full run. He followed me to the step. I shut the door and I hollered for Bessie—she was in bed—and I asked her where was the 12-gauge. She said, "What is it?" I said, "The devil is outside. A black pig, the devil, followed me," I said. She came down and says, "Where? where?" I said, "Go out." She went out, she went round the house—I was looking for the gun. I heard her squealing, making for in the house. She says, "He's there all right."

Bessie MacLeod: Ha, ha, ha, that's the truth.

John R.: Well, the door was open, the pig came in the house. What the hell was it but my neighbour's pig broke out. And he went up the mines and he rolled in the dirt, in the coal—and it all stuck to him.

Bessie: There he was sitting with the 12-gauge for to shoot his neighbour's pig. But he looked terrible. He came right in the house, yes.

John R.: I put him out, and the boys were away. They were fishing. And they were sleeping on a couch down there. And after they came home, the pig came in, in the dark, and didn't he go down and go under the couch and threw the boys on their backs out on the floor. And the hollering that was going on then. They didn't know of the pig and they didn't know of anything.

Bessie: So the neighbour came up the next day. We were after getting him out and we bolted the door. He went to the front of the house and he dug a hole for himself that deep. "My, my, my," he says, "where did my pig come from?" So he took him home. Came up with a horse and cart and took him home. But that wasn't a fairy tale.

Robert Hubbard: It was a spooky place, going up MacDonald's Glen from our place. It was about two miles up to Big Malcolm's. And the old fellow went up to visit him. Well, anytime the old fellow would go up to Big Malcolm's it'd be about two o'clock in the morning before he'd come back home. They'd get into politics and whatnot. His first door neighbour on each side of him, this night they knew he went up. And going up the glen, you see, it was all full of sluices and little bridges, you know—some of them about that high—the brook criss-crossing.

They got to the second one, the highest of them. They heard him coming. About one o'clock in the night. Dark too. They got in under the bridge. And just when he got on the bridge, they had a rock you know and they start thumping the bridge, to scare him.

And he stopped right on the bridge. He crawled on the upper side of the bridge and he got down and he lit a match and here he got the other two. Well, there was a part of a ghost business. He caught them right there. And they felt so damned rotten, they wouldn't talk to him for about two weeks. And one of them said to him, "Well, now, what would you do, Sandy, if it was the devil?"

Sandy says, "What in the hell would he be doing here?"

You take that old fellow. If he had took off at a run when the other two was under the bridge with a rock—that was a big ghost. But he discovered the ghosts.

But I am going to say this: There is such a thing as a forerunner. Yes. You can see a light all right, before a death or anything like that—or a racket. I know down home—I was only there about three years— and mostly every night at the window at the outside of the stove, there'd be a tapping there—just so much to say driving tacks. That was all right. We were thinking it was a couple of rats or something in the cellar, right below, gnawing or rattling something.

Then our first door neighbour died in 1919, with the big flu. That'd be Danny William's grandfather. So all right, it's down at our place they made his coffin. At that time there were no imported ones. They were all made home. There were two guys making the coffin. And I was looking at the coffin, you know. Well, it got late then in the evening—this was in March—it was getting cold. But they had the coffin finished only to put the cloth on—black cloth.

So all right, they took the coffin in. And I went and I laid in that coffin. No lie, now, and I never forgot it. I was about ten, I suppose. Ten or eleven. You see, he was only a very small man too. I remember him all right. I jumped in the coffin—

they were putting the clothes on—I said, "This is only big enough for me." I got an awful kick out of it. I wasn't frightened. If I was I wouldn't go in it.

But anyways, this tap-tap—you know, driving the tacks to put the black cloth on—from that night on we never heard that racket again. Never. No.

Annie MacPhee: Now at the lake there was—you remember Joe that we brought up—his grandfather was drowned in Lake Ainslie. He was a mail driver, and he was at a house—next door neighbours—this day, on a Sunday, visiting, and there was a man in there and he was double-sighted—and he could see the water dripping off him like this. He got up and he turned as white as a sheet and he walked out. And somebody followed him out and he said, "That fellow's going to be drowned yet. I could see the water dripping off him in the house"—and the man sitting talking.

So couple of years after that he was driving the mail and he had a young mare, and he just threw the reins on the fender and she took off with him—and she went over Hay's River Bridge and kept right out at the end of Hay's River Bridge out into the lake. And the mail bags were in the wagon and he had to go after her. And he swam out till he got to where she was out, and he was getting in the wagon—his coat got caught in the step of the wagon—and he went down and he was drowned. And the other fellow seen him and not a thing wrong with him—and he seen the water dripping off of him.

Bessie MacLeod: When I was home about the age of twelve or thirteen, there was one certain bed and it was one of those felt mattresses and look, there was nobody could ever sleep in that bed—you'd be turning and twisting all night long. So at the last of it that bed was put upstairs and when visitors would come and the house was full, then we'd sleep in it. When we moved, it was a very expensive mattress and I hated to throw it out, so we took it with us down here.

The children grew up then and they were complaining that they couldn't sleep in the mattress. So we shifted it from one room to another and no one would sleep in it and at last it got a tear in the felt, but I still didn't want to throw it out.

So at the end of it this old fellow across the brook died, and I was over and it was Murdock Beaton who was fixing him up. But I was over and they had nothing for packing and they asked me if I'd go home and see if I could find any cotton batting or something in the house. So I went over and I knew there was nothing there like that and I was thinking of what am I going to do. So anyways, never thinking, I spied the mattress and I said, "Here she goes, boys," and I took a stack of piling from the inside of the couch where it was torn and I took that over for the packing.

Well after that you could get a beautiful

sleep on the mattress as you would anywhere. So there you have it, that was a forerunner.

Annie MacPhee: They were saying up at John R. Beaton's in Broad Cove Marsh, that every night they'd go to sleep and the horses'd be in the barn. When they woke up in the morning, the horses' manes and tails would be all in tiny, little braids, as tight as could be. The horses would be all sweat. They were saying that the fairies would be riding the horses all night. The reasons they were braiding the hair was to make stirrups, for they were riding on the horses' necks. And if there was a lame horse or anything wrong with him, the fairies would never touch him. It was only the good ones.

I had a mare. When she was a colt, her mother wouldn't have anything to do with her, so we took her and we put her on milk, on the bucket—and she was brought up as a pet. And when she grew up she was a beautiful animal. I trained her myself, and everything about her. And dressed her and rigged her out so sporty and everything. And a cousin of mine and I went to town this day and this man used to look at her all the time, and admire her when she was in the pasture. So just as we were making the turn going up by what we call Busy Corner them days—this man met me and he said, "Look, Annie, I'll give you 350 dollars for that mare today. Just drive up back of the Co-op and I'll give you an old horse in the deal."

So I laughed. I had no intention of selling her. I said, "Double it, Mac, and you'll have her."

So I drove back and we went home that evening, everything as good as gold, nothing wrong whatsoever. Put her in the pasture. Four o'clock in the morning she landed at the door. She was so sick she was rattling the latch in the door. To attract our attention. So my uncle got up, went out, and she was rolling on the ashpile with the pain. Put her in the barn.

It cost me—in them days—over thirty-four dollars for her vet to come. The vet gave her needles and everything he could think of. And even a neighbour was making moonshine at the time. He went to the woods and he made a draw and he brought two quarts of the best moonshine—and we put that down her. Figured she had pneumonia.

Before she died, the sweat poured, it was just running down, streaming off her—and then she died. Just drew a breath and died. And this man that was around her, he asked me did I ever get an offer for the mare. I said yes, just yesterday a man offered to put a price on her. He said, "You should have sold her."

Robert Hubbard: Well, Annie, that's just the same as I know a guy, he's living today—I'll mention no names on it—and it made no difference where that man would land, if there were any kind of moving machinery or like that—something would have to break every time. Something would go. Yes.

Annie MacPhee: And I'll bet the man didn't mean or even know anything about it.

Robert: Well, we couldn't say he would.

I'll tell you a story.

There was an old woman and she was making butter, she was selling the butter. Well, I guess the store she would take the butter to, he couldn't get rid of it. I guess the butter was pretty *ropach*, not manufactured good enough to sell. So he'd only give her about half the price that the other women would get.

After a while she found out about this. She asked the storekeeper this day, "How is it that I don't get full price same as the other women." "Well," he said, "I might as well tell you."

So he told her that her butter was still in the back of the shop there and can't get rid of it unless he sells it for cart grease, putting it on cart axles. "Well," she said to herself, "I guess the butter'll be good and clean the next time."

There was a brook ran below the house and there was a big flat rock there with a kind of a hollow in it. She made the churn and took the butter down. She laid it on the rock in the brook. Took her shoes off and got into it with her feet. Start cleaning it, you know, the butter—get out the buttermilk. By god she slipped and come down on her arse in it.

"Aw," she said, "butter at the old price! Butter at the old price!"

When the Party Danced to Thread

by Winston "Scotty" Fitzgerald

My father couldn't even buy a set of strings sometimes. I remember being at a place one night, and we had no violin. No fiddle. And there were enough gathered at the house for a party. Had a pot of molasses candy. So, something was said, "Too bad we don't have a fiddle—Winston would play for a square set." Which would take eight—four boys and four girls.

"By God," I said, "got a piece of board around, a box or something?" So they went and they got a piece of box, something like a crate, an orange crate or something. And we got a piece of wood. And we got a spool of black thread. I can see it yet.

And rigged it up. And the little boys went out and got an alder—elder—alder, I call it—switch. And we put the black thread on it from end to end. And a piece of spruce gum off a tree—that's what I had for rosin.

And help me God, everybody took their shoes off, you know, or you wouldn't hear it. It wasn't very loud. But we had three or four square sets there—and I made the fiddle and played. God is my judge. You know, that's hard to believe, isn't it?

You'd almost think a fellow made that up, but that's true.

At the Glengarry Mineral Springs

told by Stephen W. MacNeil

I was born right here (on the Glengarry Road at Big Pond) in 1901. And The Spring—it seems that the last settler out on this road, about seven miles from here anyway—he was after his cattle; you know, bringing his cattle home in the evening. Hector MacIntyre, that was the fellow that found The Spring. The cattle stopped at this place—a little brook there too—and he saw them drinking this water. And he went to investigate what it was, and he saw this spring there; he could see the water pumping up from way down. And he was crippled with rheumatism—he had to walk with a cane and all that—old man, too, I guess, at the time—and he tasted the water and the taste was terrible, you know, salty and hard to drink. So he drank it anyways. He thought there might be a cure in it for his rheumatism.

And the next day he went back after the cows, or with them again, and he drank some more of it. And in three or four days drinking this spring water, he threw the cane away—he was cured. And he found out it was the water, the mineral water, that cured him. And he advertised it and told what happened—and then he was a busy man keeping people away, because they were passing his door going to the spring, a lot of them getting cured. That's how the thing started....

I can tell the story of a man who came here. He was from Waterford, a cripple, and his hands were swollen and he had a rubber on one foot and a shoe on the other. And he came—it was horse-and-wagon days, before motor—and he asked, could he stay for the night. He told his condition and that he was going to the Mineral Spring.

Well, we tried to get him out of the wagon and he just made it in the house somehow, and we had supper. He just came at supper time. He sat at the table with us, or with me anyway—I was only very young—and I had to peel the potatoes for him and butter his bread and did everything for him. He could lift the cup to his mouth, that was all. And he told us his story, that if he could get another horse, would we give him a horse to take him out to the Spring while he'd rest his horse, next day, you know.

We had a bed and we put him in bed, and the next day we tried to go. I got my own horse and put it on his wagon and was going with him, but when we got everything ready, he couldn't get up in the wagon. I had to go down for my uncle below the road here. He came up and the two of us helped to get him in the wagon—he was that crippled—and I took him out.

Oh, it was a real hot day, very hot, but we got to the Spring, and got him out of the wagon somehow, and he took off all his clothes excepting his underwear, and he bathed. You couldn't bail but about 2 1/2 gallons. You'd bail that out, then she'd fill again 2 1/2 more gallons. So we finally got enough and he got me to soak him.

He laid down in the sun and I soaked him all over with his underwear on, you know. And he drank some of it too. And I went off wandering and he was there, and I came back and the underwear was quite dry. He says, "Soak me again with it; put it all over me." Soaked him again. He had a nice little hill there. And he drank it again. Then he had jars, the old-fashioned jars, I believe he had two of those. We started filling the jars. He was going to take that with him.

Sunday was the next day. He wanted me to go out with him again Sunday. Well, I decided I would, doing the same thing for him. He seemed to have money—he was very free talking about it anyway—I'd make a dollar for myself. Anyway, we got him supper and same as before, I buttered the bread for him and everything. He couldn't do anything. He went to bed and everybody went to bed.

And the next morning, we were going to church. It was only I and Mother home at that time—the rest of them were gone, I guess—so we didn't bother to wake him, you know, left him in bed because he wasn't able to do anything or take anything. And we went to church and we came home after Mass—he was after getting up. And he'd had his breakfast—he did it all himself—bread and an egg or two and whatever it was that was going at the time. And, "Look," he says, "I'm pretty near all right." "Will we go out to Glengarry?" "No," he says, "I don't think it's necessary. I'm going to be all right. But anyway," he said, "I'll stay. I didn't intend to go back 'til Monday anyway, so I'll stay here and we'll go out Monday if I'm no better."

My god, he could butter his bread, he could peel potatoes, and he could feed himself. It was a wonderful change to what it was. And sure enough, he stayed all day. He washed himself with some of the five gallons, and he was in the sun there. He stayed around all day Sunday, and Monday we were supposed to go up again but we never went. And he got the wagon and helped hitch the horse, and about a week afterwards we got a letter from him—he was working in the pit. He was a coal miner.

There's a lot of other people dead and gone now that could tell you the same of miracles that happened out there. Cures, wonderful cures.

(Did prayer play any role in this?) Well I don't think, as far as this man was concerned. I never heard him say a word about God while he was here. (Would the priest ever talk about the waters out there?) Well, the old priests that were here before my time were supposed to have blessed it and things like that, but I never heard of priests predicting that it cured.

I think it was the stuff in the water, if there was cure in it. It must have been effective. My

98

aunt also. She was terrible with rheumatism. She was a bed patient for a long time, and there was a doctor in Sydney that recommended the Spring to her. She got better, anyway. I don't know if she was drinking it or rubbing it or what she was doing, but she was on her feet in a few days. Rheumatism. That was about the only thing I heard that it would cure.

When the Truck Went Through the Ice

told by Mickey MacLean

I've been crossing on the ice twenty-five or thirty years. There were one or two winters in the early '30s, we didn't have any ice—you couldn't cross the lake. But we've crossed the ice there and the wind has smashed it up the next day.

I crossed over here on the 6th of January. And I was just within a couple of hundred feet from the other side, and I happened to look down the lake and I saw the gypsum boat coming—so I thought I'd better get back to this side. I got back. There was four inches of good ice—good hard ice—aw, the boat went through it like there was nothing there. And there hasn't been any come since.

That was this year.

A year ago, I went over on the ice—I think it was on the 7th I walked over and on the 15th I went over with the car—just a week afterwards, I went over with the car.

(Do a lot of people do that?) Not too many. None went last year but myself. There was one other car. The first time I came on the ice was 1917-18, time I came to Baddeck with my father. They were hauling hay. And I don't think I missed too many winters since—not any that I know of, clear of the winter that we didn't have any.

I put a truck through the ice out there once. I got in a pond and I couldn't get out of it. There was snow on it. It was a pond back of Kidston's Island. A wheel hooked in the pond and it pulled me into the pond. I had no chains. Too slippery, I couldn't get out. I got out of her, let her go. She eventually sunk.

But I got her out of there some days afterward. Cut a hole, some holes, and put down a cable. Got a diver to go down, put a cable on her. Pulled her in on the island. Cleaned the motor out. They were all telling me the motor would be ruined.

(*How was she?*) All right. She was never— she never had too much power in second gear. She was lazy. When she got that cleaning out, there wasn't a hill in Washabuck or Iona but she'd fly over it. Cleaned her right out.

Lauchie and the August Gale

told by H. L. Livingstone

I've written up one on my uncle, who was the only survivor of the August Gale (1873) in the Gulf of St. Lawrence.

Lauchie was a young man in his early thirties when he returned from the American Civil War. He took his place in his father's shipyard at Big Bras d'Or. That was my grandfather, Sandy Livingstone. Lauchie was the younger son of Sandy, the shipbuilder, and he had helped to build a ship called the *John Lauchlin*. This was the last one, I think, they built in the shipyard at Big Bras d'Or. And she was possibly a double-ender. I'm not sure of that—but she was very broad in the beam and very high in the bow and stern. That impeded her speed but made her very seaworthy.

You've heard about the August Gale, Nova Scotia's biggest storm. Well, Lauchie was coming down from the west coast of Newfoundland with a cargo of dried fish from Bonne Bay and Bay of Islands—and the hurricane hit when he was somewhere near St. Paul's Island, just north of St. Paul's. He tried to tack into Sydney under a reefed foresail—but about eleven o'clock in the morning the foresail blew away—a new sail just put on the ship—the foresail blew away.

And then they put out a sea anchor. The wind was so strong and the sea so high that the rope kept breaking on the sea anchor. And, afraid that he would lose members of the crew overboard, he stopped it and raced before the hurricane.

Well, he began to think seriously about what would happen. Because here he was in the Gulf of St. Lawrence without sea room—the worst position that a sailor can find himself in. If he has a good ship, the only thing a sailor fears in a hurricane is land. He knew if the storm lasted all night he would be driven ashore on the coast of New Brunswick or on the north side of Prince Edward Island, because he was racing northwestward, right in the Gulf.

So about noon he went on deck. He had gone below when the sea anchor was carried away. He went on deck, he ordered all hands below, battened down the hatches, lashed himself to the wheel, and he deliberately put his ship broadside to the storm. Something you're never supposed to do with a sailing ship, because if she has sails and wind in her sails it keeps her rather steady, although she'll lean over. But without sails she rolls until she rolls completely over.

About four o'clock that afternoon he couldn't see the foremast through the drifting spray. The hurricane was almost 100 miles an hour, with spray drifting off the tops of the waves. And every time she would fall away and start to race before the hurricane, he'd put the wheel hard over and bring her up into the sea again. Broadside to the storm.

Below decks I guess everybody thought that he'd gone crazy, because she was rolling so badly—but that set the broad keel of the *John Lauchlin* to the tide, so that it cut down her rate of drift. He made a complete wide circle around the Magdalen Islands. And daylight found him just north of the northeast tip of Prince Edward Island. So he ran in under a headland. The wind was by that time going down.

He brought the crew on deck. Rigged up a spare foresail and came into North Sydney three days later—the only ship in the Gulf of St. Lawrence that survived. More than 1000 persons drowned on this coast and the coast of P.E.I. in that storm. In Arichat alone, as Capt. Parker points out in *Cape Breton Ships and Men*, fifty heads of families were never heard from again.

So Lauchie, being stubborn, non-conformist, refused to believe what the rule book said, and saved the ship and its crew.

And while the storm was at its height and the trees were being uprooted around my grandfather's little log house at Big Bras d'Or—my grandmother said, "I'm afraid about poor Lauchie if he's in this." My grandfather said, "Don't worry about him. He'll know just what to do in any storm. Lauchie's got a good ship and the ship's got a good master." And it did.

The Man Who Was Caught Changing

re-told by Archie Neil Chisholm

Now, you go down among the Acadian people and they will tell you the exact same thing. They used to claim that many of the old women—I forget, it wasn't quite what you'd call a *sorcier*, a witch or a wizard—but they had those people in Cheticamp. And it was very common, particularly in the early days, in the days when the Jerseys first came in, that many of the French people believed that the Jerseys had supernatural powers. And one man, I will give you his name, Lubie Chiasson, I had him up here when I was doing the program "Archie Neil's Cape Breton." And Lubie educated me that night with stories of the things that used to be done by the Jerseys.

And there was one particular wizard there who had put an evil spell and a curse on you and his name was Charlie. Lubie told me that his father used to fish for the Jerseys. And that was before Father Fiset's time. And his father was always poor and he got married and he lived in a shack and he wanted to build a house. He had lumber. He could get the lumber and he could saw it with a rip-saw but the one thing that (was hard for) him was to get the nails.

Now Lubie told me that one day his father

was down on the shore standing on the wharf and he heard a noise beneath the wharf. And there was this Charlie turning himself—now, remember, these are stories, I'm not telling you as a fact; but Lubie would tell it as a fact—Charlie was converting himself into an animal. They were supposed to have this ability to transfer themselves from one body to another. And he was in the midst of this when Mr. Chiasson looked down at him.

Now one of the things that they could not do was if they were caught, if you kept your eye on them, they couldn't keep changing—they'd have to remain in the condition they were in. So Charlie told the old man—well, he wasn't an old man then—to go away and the old man said he wouldn't. And then Charlie said, "What do you want? I'll give you what you want if you'll go away." And he says, "I want a promise that you'll give me the nails to build my house." And when he did the old man went away and Charlie turned himself into whatever animal he wished to be for the time being.

The next day Chiasson went down to the store that they had then and Charlie gave him the nails on the condition that he wouldn't tell anyone while he was living that he saw him converting himself into another creature. Now, that happened, oh, probably a hundred years ago and Lubie was able to tell it because both his father and Charlie were long dead when Lubie told that on my program. If you were to look in Father Anselme

Chiasson's *History of Cheticamp* you will find page after page after page of this material that I'm giving you right now. Different stories and different curses and different beliefs that they had. And one of the things that they believed in was the fact that the Jerseymen had supernatural powers.

Editor's Note: This story was collected by Linda MacLellan of Belle Côte. Sticking to the courtesies and restrictions of his own traditions, Archie Neil told Linda this story of "changing form" as he would properly tell it to a woman. On another occasion, Archie Neil told a man about the same event. The difference was that Charlie was seen under the bridge turning himself into a bull. And later, after the deal for the nails was made, Charlie was seen completely transformed into a bull, heading off for a pasture full of cows.

The Yarning Old Men of Strawberry Glen

by Archibald J. MacKenzie

(English begins on page 115)

Nuair a fhuair mi churachd seachad, na caoirich air an rusgadh, an spreigh air an cuir am fearachas, agus deise us boineid ùr a cheannach do Sheonaid; thuirt mi rium fhein, "A bhodaich ma tha thu glic, 'se so an t-àm airson na raimh a tharruinn a stigh agus cead iarraidh air Seonaid gu dol latha no dha air cheilidh do Ghleann Na Suidheag." Bha fios agam nach bu mhisde mo chàs beagan do bhial briagha a thoirt dhi an toiseach. 'S ann air a shon fhein a ni an cat an cronan, agus thuirt mi: "A Sheonaid a ghraidh, nach cuir thu ort an deise ùr 'sa bhonaid a fhuair mi dhuit feuch am faic mi de cho boidheach sa sheallas tu leotha."

"Ni mi sin," ars' ise.

Ann an tiota bha i na culaidh agus gu firinneach, ged 's mi fhin a tha ga radh, bha i sealltainn eireachdail. "Nach mi bhios leomach nuair a sheasas tu ri 'm ghuallain 'san eaglais Didomhnuich. Cha bhi te eile cho dreachmhor ruit ann. Tha thu cheart cho eireachdail an diugh sa bha thu an latha phos sinn. Nach i Mairi an Dosain fhein an deagh bhan-taillear? Sin agad a nisd deise, 's cha ne na feilean beaga a chi thu air nigheanan an latha an diugh. Gu meal 's gu'n caith

107

thu i. Gu dearbh 's mi a fhuair an deagh bhargain an latha a fhuair mi thu air da dhollar."

"De tha thu ciallachadh?" ars' ise.

"Tha gu'm be da dhollar a thug mi da'n t-sagart choir a phos sinn."

"Stad ort," ars' ise, "cha robh sin cho math ris an bhargain a rinn mise nuair a fhuair mi an duine 's coire agus a's fhearr anns an duthaich a'n asgaidh."

"Fuirich samhach a Sheonaid, ma chluinne-as Murchadh Boisgeil sin gheibh e bas leis an ta-mailt. Tha e tinn gu leoir on latha phos sinn. Ach am bheil fios agad a Sheonaid, gu'm bu toigh leam latha no dha fhaighinn dhomh fhin go dol a chei-lidh air mo luchd eolais am Baile na Suidheag.

"De do bharail, an rachadh agad fhein agus na balaich air gach ni a chumail air doigh fhad 's a bhithinn air falbh?"

"An ann a dol a choimhead do sheann lean-nan Mor nan Gag a tha thu? Chuala mi thu an de a toirt smuid air seinn a phuirt aice, 'So am baile 's a bheil a bhoile 's na fir an deaghaidh Mor nan Gag.' Ma 's ann cuiridh mise fios air Gille na Mo-gan tighinn 'nad aite fhad sa bhios tu air falbh. Faodadh tu falbh amaireach a ghraidh agus cha churam dhuinn go'n till thu."

Dh'fhag mi a' seinn air mo rathad:

Moch sa mhaduinn rinn mi gluasad,
'S thilg mi an t-seachaid air mo ghuallain.

Thilg mi an t-seachaid air mo ghuallain,

108

'S thug mi bata do fhiodh cruaidh leam.

Thug mi bata do fhiodh cruaidh leam,
'S a righ bu sgairteil bha mo ghluasad.

Righ bu sgairteil bha mo ghluasad
A h-uile ceum dol na bu luaithe.

A h-uile ceum dol na bu luaithe,
C'ait ro'n gaisgeach chuma suas rium.

C'ait ro'n gaisgeach chuma suas rium.
Direadh bheann 's a tearnadh chruachan.

Direadh bheann sa tearnadh chruachan,
Dol dan ghleann sa'm bheil na h-uaislean.

Dol da'n ghleann sa'm bheil na h-uaislean,
Ghleidh a Ghadhlig sa thug luaidh dhi.

Bha an oidhche ann nuair a rainig mi an Gleann agus ghabh mi go taigh Thearlaich Chrotaich far am bu tric a fhuair mi caoimhneas agus a dh'eisd mi ri naigheachdan, garbh agus ait. Bhuail mi aig an dorus agus thainig Tearlach coir go fhosgladh. "Dia a bhi ann an so," arsa mi-fhin. "Dia dhut fhein," ars' easan. "An e an gille fada tha so?" "Se," arsa mise, "ach nam biodh a chroit agaibh fhein air a direachadh, bhiodh sibh a cheart cho fada rium-sa." "Gabh leis an sin an drasda agus dean suidhe, 's math an oidhche thainig thu. Tha comhdail gu bhi aig Comunn na Firinn an so a nochd agus bi-thidh sinn toilichte thu bhi 'nar cuideachd."

Co a thainig a stigh aig a cheart àm ach Ru-

airidh Dubh, Seumas Mor, agus Domhnull Sunndach. 'S mise a fhuair an crathadh làmh, cha mhor
nach d'thug Domhnull Sunndach dhion i! "Tha thu
cho sunndach sa bha thu riabh a Dhomhnuill," arsa mise. "Nach e sin fhein an doigh cheart," ars'
easan. "De a feum ann a bhi trom-inntinneach, sin
galair a dh'fhagas neach caol."

'S tric a bha mi cuimhneachadh nuair a bha
sinn a dol do'n sgoil a liuthad cuil-bheairt a rinn
sinn. "Am bheil cuimhne agad an latha a chuir
sinn an losgann anns an mhalaid aig Iain Gagach
ro am a dhinneir? Sin far an robh na leadain. Cha
chuala Sagan fhein riabh a leithid!"

A nis bha toil agam stad a chuir air Domhnull mu'n innseadh e an corr de na cuil-bheairtean
a rinn sinn, agus thuirt mi ris, "Nach ann a bha
latha teth an diugh?" "Teth," arsa Tearleach. "Na
faice tu an latha teth a chunnaic mise, be sin an
latha bha teth. Tha mi cinnteach nach eil cuimhne
aig aon agaibhse air, ach 's math mo chuimhne-sa
air an latha.

"Bha mi-fhin agus m'athair a reiteach coille
dhubh anns an robh sinn a' dol a chur buntata. 'S
ann goirid do Feill Peadair a bh'ann. Bha latha
ciuin samhach, gu'n neoil ri fhaicinn air an adhar
agus teas ann a bha gun chiall. Mar 's math tha fios agaibh 'se coille dhubh nuair tha teas mor ann
aite 's teoidhe air an t-saoghal. Bha sinn a cuir na
maidean 's gach smodal eile na'n torran an sid sa
so, bha am fallus gar dalladh's ar casan ga losgadh.
Mu aon uair deug, mar urchair as gunna, chaidh

na terran na'n teine, 's b-fheudar dhuinn teicheadh go an abhuinn. Sin far robh an sealladh, bha an t-uisge cho teth 's gu'n robh na bric a leam go tir!"

"Tha mi cinnteach," arsa mise, "gu'm faca sibh lathaichean a bha anabarrach fuar cuideachd?" "Fuar. Oi 's mise chunnaic sin," ars Tearlach. "Chunnaic mise latha cho fuar 's gu'n do reoidh Loch Mhor Bhra-Dor cho ealamh 's nach d'fhuair nan stuadhan laidhe sios. Bha stoirm mhor ann o'n Ear Thuath 's bha a'n fhairge anabarrach ard, ach ged bha sin mar sin, reoidh na stuadhan na'n seasamh. Fhearaibh, fhearaibh, sid an latha bha ainmeil! 'S a mhaduinn an ath latha, dh'fhalbh mi null air gnothach do'n bhuth aig Niall Ruairidh Phearsainn 's a Phon Mhor. Thug mi leam an tuagh 's an t-sleighe. Cha deach mi fada mach air an deigh nuair a thachair trosg mor rium, reoidhte ann am barr na'n stuadh. Ghearr mi às an deigh e agus chuir mi air an t-sleighe e. Ach cha deach mi fad air aghairt gus na thachair fear is fear eile rium, gus na lion mi an t-sleighe leo, agus b'iad sin na truisg! Cha robh aon fo shia troidhean a dh'fhad. Reic mi iad ri Niall Ruairi iad agus fhuair mi prìs mhath orra. Air mo thurus dhachaidh chuir mi cruach eile do'n trosg air an t-sleighe, agus be sin iasgach bu mhotha a rinn aon duine riabh sa an duthaich so ann an aon latha, agus 's mise rinn e leis an tuagh. Sin agaibh a nisd smior na firinn oir 's mise Ceann-fheadhna Comunn na Firinn."

"An robh buntata math agaibh 's a choille

dhubh a chaidh na teine le teas na greine?"
dh'fharraid mise. "Bha gle mhath," ars easan.
"Rinn a h-uile torran leth buseil." "Cha chanainn-
sa," arsa Seumas Mor, "buntata math ris a sin. 'S
ann a bha am buntata math agamsa a cheud bhli-
adhna a chuir mi na Girlings, agus 's ann an coille
dhubh a bha iad agam. Nuair a thainig àm an togail dh'fhalbh mi fhin agus na gillean aon latha
agus thug sinn leinn na daimh, sleighe agus poca-
nan gus am buntata thoirt go'n taigh. Ach a chair-
dean cha do chuir sinn aon bhuntata ann am poca
fad an latha. Bha iad cho mor agus gur e a rinn
sinn an cuir air fad air an t-sleighe eadar na sta-
nardan, mar a bhitheamaid a cuir an chonnadh.
Nuair a bha mi-fhin a fas sgith a g'obair de a thachair rium ach buntata anns an robh dusan troidh
a dh'fhad agus gairbhead da reir. Chladhaich mi
mu'n cuairt dha ach cha b'urrain dhomh car a
chuir dheth gu's an d'thainig na gillean gu'm chui-
deachadh le inneal togail. Nuair a chuir sinn car
dheth a nuas as an toll, leum a mhuc mhor a bha
air chall orm fad an t-samhraidh agus dusan do
uirceanan a mach as a thaobh. Sin agaibh far an
robh am buntata."

"Tha iad ag radh gu'n robh coille uamhasach
mor air an aite agaibhse, Sheumais." "Bha sin air
a charaid, mar a theid agam air a dhearbhadh
dhutsa. 'S math mo chuimhne air aon chraobh a
bh'ann. Thug mi-fhin agus an Griasaiche tri latha
gu gearradh mu'n do thuit i, agus nuair a bhuail i
an talamh, chrith e cho mor agus gu'n do bhrist a

112

h-uile uinneag a bh'ann an tighean a ghlinne. Dh'fhalbh pios mor do bheinn Cobh Nam Piopaire- an a mach da'n mhuir, agus thuit Bean Dhomh- nuil Shaoir a mach as an leaba urlair anns an robh i na sineadh."

"Nach bu mhath an t-each a thairneadh i," arsa Domhnull Sunndach. "Bha each aig m'athair- sa thairneadh i gu ealamh," arsa Ruairidh Dubh, "agus chunnaic mis' e deanamh gniomh fada bu duillighe. Bha an t-ait aig m'athair air taobh sli- abh suas on chuan. Latha bha sid, bha mi-fhin agus m'athair a treabhadh leis an each mhor suas on chladach. Mu leth mile a mach on chladach bha tanalach air nach robh a bheag do uisge. Chunna- ic sinn long mhor a ruith ro'n t-soirbheas agus a stuireadh direach air an tanalach. 'Co an t- amadan a tha na cheannard air a'n iuraich iad?' arsa m'athair. 'Tha e dol gu cuir ann an leaba as nach toir esan i.' Mar a thuirt b'fhior. Ghabh a long suas air an tanalaich 's cha mhor nach do bhrist na cruinn dhi. Leag iad no siuil 's dh'fhiach iad gach innleachd a bha na'n comas gus a toirt far na tanalach ach cha ghluaiseadh a'n iurach.

"Thainig an Caiphtein go tir far an robh sinn agus bha e ann an staid thruagh, an sileadh na'n diar mu'n chall a thainig air. Dh'fharraid m'athair dheth co as an robh e agus thuirt e gu'n robh e a Sasunn. 'Dh'aighnich mi sin,' arsa m'athair. 'Nam bu Ghaidheal thusa cha toireadh tu suas an cas gus a fartlicheadh e ort seachd turuis. Ach am bheil capall laidir fada agad air bord?' 'Tha,' ars easan. 'Bi falbh mata,' arsa m'athair, 'agus faigh e deiseil. Theid mise a mach as do dheidh agus chi sinn de theid againn air a dheanamh.'

"Dh'fhuasgail e an t-each on chrann-treabha, cheangal e na treasachan ris na claragan, leum e air druim a'n eich 's a mach a ghabh iad air an t-snamh gu'n long. Bha e muigh troimh an Chaiph-tein; agus nuair fhuair e ceann a chapall chean-gail e ris an amull e, agus thug e aghaidh an eich a mach da'n chuan. Chuir e na spuirean na thaobh, 's a mach a ghabh an t-each leis an luinng gus na dh'fhag e i air uisge sabhailte. Sin agaibh a nisd each a bha laidir," arsa Ruairidh Dubh.

The Yarning Old Men of Strawberry Glen

re-told by Norman MacDonald

As soon as I had finished the sowing, sheared the sheep, put the cattle out to pasture, and bought a new suit and hat for Jessie, I said to myself, "Old man, if you are wise this is the day to pull in the oars and ask Jessie's permission to go for a day or two to visit the Glen of the Strawberries." I knew well that it would do no harm to speak sweetly to her before raising the matter, as it's for his own ends that the cat purrs. I said, "Jessie, my darling, won't you put on the new dress and hat which I bought for you, so that I can see how beautiful you look in them."

"I'll do that," she said. In a moment she was dressed, and, truth to tell, though I say it myself, she looked elegant.

"Won't I be proud when you stand at my shoulder in Church on Sunday. There will not be another there as beautiful as you. You are just as elegant today as you were on the day we married. Is not Mairi an Dossain the fine tailor-woman? That, now, is a suit, rather than the short dresses you see on today's girls. May you enjoy and wear it. Indeed, it was I who got the bargain the day I got you for two dollars."

"What do you mean?" she asked.

"I mean that it was two dollars I gave the kind priest who married us."

"Take it easy," she said, "that was not as good as the bargain I struck the day I got the best and the kindest man in the district free of charge."

"Stay silent, Jessie, if Murchadh Boisgeil hears that he'll die of humiliation. He has been sick enough since the day we married. But do you know, Jessie, that I would like to get a day or two for myself to go visit my acquaintances in the Glen of the Strawberries.

"What do you think? Do you suppose you and the boys could keep everything going while I would be away?"

"Is it to visit your old sweetheart Mor nan Gag that you are going? I heard you yesterday, heartily singing her tune, 'This is the town in which there is passion and the men after Mor nan Gag.' If it is, I will send word to the boys of Mogan to come and replace you while you are away. You can go tomorrow, my darling, and we will have no worries until you return."

I left, singing on my way:

Early one morning I set out
Throwing my jacket on my shoulder

Throwing my jacket on my shoulder
And taking with me a hardwood cane,

Taking with me a hardwood cane,
And, King, how vigorous was my movement.

King, how vigorous was my movement
With each step the pace quickening.

With each step the pace quickening,
Where was the hero who could keep up?

Where was the hero who could keep up?
Climbing hills and descending bens,

Climbing hills and descending bens,
Going to the Glen where the nobles dwell

Going to the Glen where the nobles dwell
Who maintained the Gaelic and who praised it.

It was night when I reached the Glen and I went to the house of Tearlach Crotach where I often received kindness and where I listened to tales, fierce and funny. I knocked on the door and kind Tearlach came to open it. "Thank God, to be here," said I. "Thank God, for yourself," said he. "Is this the tall boy?" "It is," said I, "but if your hump was straightened, you would be just as tall as I."

"That's enough of that just now and sit down, for you've come on a good night. The Association of Truth are to have a convention here tonight and we will be very happy for you to join us."

Who should come in the door at that precise moment but Ruairidh Dubh, Seumas Mor, and Domhnull Sunndach. I certainly received warm hand-shakes, so much so that Domhnull Sunndach almost removed my hand! "You are as cheerful as ever you were, Domhnull," I said. "Isn't that the right way," said he. "What good is it to be dejected, for that's a disease that will leave a man thin."

Often did I think of the tricks we played on our way to school. "Do you remember," Domhnull asked, "the day we put the frog in Iain Gagach's satchel before lunch? That's when we heard the litanies! Satan himself never heard the likes of it!"

Now, I wished to stop Domhnull before he'd tell any more of the tricks we played, and I said to him, "Wasn't it a hot day, today?" "Hot!?" said Tearlach. "If you'd seen the hot day I saw, now that was a hot day. I'm sure none of you remember that day.

"My father and I were out clearing black forest in which we were going to plant potatoes. It was near St. Patrick's Day. The day was calm and still, with not a cloud to be seen in the sky. And heat that was without sense. As you well know, the black forest on a hot day is the hottest place in the world. We were putting the branches and all other debris in piles here and there, the sweat was blinding us, and our feet were near to burning. About eleven o'clock, like a bullet from a gun, the piles went on fire, and we had to retreat to the river. That's where we saw the sight! The water was so hot that the trout were jumping to land!"

"I am sure," said I, "that you also saw days which were extremely cold?" "Cold!? O, yes, it's I that saw that," said Tearlach. "I saw a day so cold that the Big Bras d'Or lake froze so hard that the waves did not get an opportunity to lie down. There was a big storm from the North-West and the seas were very high, but although that was the case, the waves froze standing. Men, men, that was the day that was noteworthy! Next morning, I went over on an errand to Niall Ruairidh Phearsainn's store in Big Pond. I took with me the axe and the sleigh. I had not gone far out on the ice when I met a large cod frozen on the top of the waves. I cut it free from the ice and put it on the sleigh. But I had not gone far before I met another, then another, until I filled the sleigh with them, and they were some cod! There was not one under six foot in length. I sold them to Niall Ruairi and got a good price for them. On my way home, I put another pile of the cod on the sleigh and that was the biggest fishing that one man ever made in one day in this district, and it was I who did it with the axe. That is now for you the essence of the truth, as I am the Chief of the Association of Truth."

"Did you have good potatoes in the black forest which went on fire?" I asked. "We had, very good," he replied. "Every sheaf produced half a bushel."

"I would not," said Seumas Mor, "call that big potatoes. It was I who had the big potatoes the first year I planted the Girlings, and it was in a black forest that I had them. When the time to lift them came, the boys and I went one day and we took with us the oxen, sleigh, and bags in which to bring the potatoes to the house. But, my friends, we put not one potato in a bag all day. They were so large that what we did was to put them all on the sleigh between the sticks as we would do with the firewood. As I was getting tired working, what should I meet but one potato measuring a dozen feet in length with appropriate width. I dug round about it, but I could not turn it until the boys came to help me with lifting apparatus. When we turned it up out of the hole, the sow which had been missing on me all summer jumped, with a dozen piglets, out of a hole beside it. That's where there was the potato.

"They say there was a very big forest on your place, Seumas."

"There was indeed, my friend, as I can prove to you. Well I remember one tree on it. The shoemaker and I spent three days cutting it before it fell. And when it hit the ground, it shook so much that it broke every window in the houses in the glen. A large part of Piper's Cove Mountain went out to sea, and Domhnall Saor's wife fell out of the floor bed on which she was lying."

"Wouldn't it be a good horse that would pull her?" said Domhnull Sunndach.

"My father had a horse that would pull her wonderfully," said Ruairidh Dubh, "and I saw it performing an act much more difficult. My father's place was on the side of a mountain rising up from the ocean. One day, my father and I were ploughing with the big horse above the shore. About half a mile out from the shore there was a stretch of shallow water. We saw a large ship sailing directly for the shallow water. 'Who is the fool who is in charge of that vessel?' asked my father. 'He is going to put her in a bed out of which he will not be able to take her.' As said, it happened. The ship sailed up the shallow and the mast almost broke off her. They lowered the sails and tried every device in their power to move her but the vessel would not move.

"The Captain came ashore where we were but he was in a poor state, and weeping about the loss that had stricken him. My father asked him where he was from and he replied that he was from England. 'I knew that,' said my father. 'If you were a Highlander you would not give up the fight until you had failed seven times. But do you have a long, strong cable on board?' 'I do have,' he replied. 'Be off with you, then,' said my father, 'and prepare it. I will go out after you and we'll see what we can do.'

"He opened the horse from the plough, tied the tresses to the frame, jumped on top of the horse and out they went, swimming to the vessel. He was out before the Captain and when he got to the end of the cable, he tied it to the yoke and directed the horse's head out to sea. He put the spurs in his side and the horse took off with the vessel until he had reached safe water. That, now, was a horse that was strong," said Ruairidh Dubh.

END of "Yarning Old Men"

The Margaree River in Flood

told by Jimmy Hannigan

If the water was anyways good shape at all, more fish would come in. (What do you mean by good shape?) Well, I mean if the water was up a good high. Say right now the water is terrible low. Awful low. And it gets warm and the fish don't like it as well. But when there's a freshet, a big rain, it cleans the river out and it makes clean water— good cold water for the fish—and they'll come right in.

And I'll tell you another thing that's hurting our rivers today—at least in my opinion of it—is lumber woods. (How do you mean?) Well, it won't hold the snow. Where they cut all those woods off miles of it around, the snow in the spring melts as fast as it can.

I remember in St. Ann's—I worked in there with twelve feet of snow. (*In among the trees?*) Yes. Well, you see, that'd take it probably two months to melt. Which kept the river up high. But now it'll wash right out once you get hot weather. There's nothing to hold that snow.

And the same with the rain when it's raining: the shade of those trees cooled the ground and it wouldn't go down in the ground so much—it would run off to the river when the ground was wet enough. But today it's got nothing—it's just like a prairie—just dry land now.

We used to get big freshets one time. We don't get them any more. We don't get the water. This here farm was all washed out one time with a freshet when we had a sawmill here. Over there— that was the mill dam out that flat there. And this high water came and the dam broke out, and we lost a lot of lumber, and it undermined the barn that was down there, too. The only thing that held the barn was the piers on the centre of the barn— they held—and it was rocking like that.

There was a cow and a yearling and the horse in the barn. And the flooring that the cow was on wasn't spiked—and they floated from under her. And she broke the rope she was tied to and swam out underneath the sill of the barn. We had a pile of slabs out there—it was about fifteen feet high—and that was the only thing she could see clear of the mountain. And she made for that. And she got up on that. Well, she couldn't get off it, and she was stranded on the slab pile.

And we got a rope on the yearling—oh, the water—there was about ten feet of water out along there—it started undermining the house at that corner, dug a hole over eight feet deep. It was lucky it didn't hurt the house any, kept working out. And we got the yearling and pulled him through the water and got him in the house here. When the water was high, we thought the house was going to go. My father took my mother and the three of us and got us on the side of the bank and down to my grandfather's—he lived down below.

And he came back here, and the next morning there were three or four fellows from up the road came down with ropes. My father got the ropes on himself, and went out and got them on the cow, and they pulled the cow off the slab pile and over through the water to the house.

And the road down below here at the end of this field—that whole side of that mountain came down, shut the road off, shut the brook off and everything—they had to build a road across over the top of the mountain to get out of here in the winter.

(*And that's because of how much water came down the Margaree River at one time?*) Yeah. (*And today?*) You never see it coming up over the banks hardly. Very seldom. No, it was an awful freshet. (*But it made for a better salmon river?*) Yes. Yes.

Marguerite Gallant Tells Little Stories

People ask me, what do you do when you're alone? Well, sometimes I tell myself stories, sometimes I sing, sometimes I remember all the old jokes in the olden time.

Listen. Oh, this was years and years ago. I suppose I wasn't even born. They were having a party. And they were crying for liquor. And look, my cousin, that fellow could steal the eyes out of your head. They said to him, "You haven't got any brains." He said, "If you give me two dollars I'll give you all the rum you want." And an old man in Margaree used to sell rum. And this night, I suppose it was a night like tonight, I suppose it was kind of stormy. So there comes my cousin, a knock at the door. He said, "I saw your light shining and I was so cold, I thought I'd come in and say how do you do to you." And he says, "That's not all." He says, "Years ago you sold me a bottle of rum, and I didn't pay for it. "Oh," the old man said, "that isn't anything." "Oh," my cousin said, "I came in on purpose to pay you." "Well," the old man says, "you're an honest man."

Then after he got warmed up, he stood to button his coat, the old man said, "Aren't you going to buy another bottle of rum?" "Oh well," he said, "that two dollars was all I had. I have no more money." "Well then," the old man said, "I'll give you all the rum you want to take home, because you are an honest man." Well, he went back to St. Joseph du Moine there and they had the time of their life, for two dollars.

(*Margie, were you ever in love?*) Well, of course I was in love. But you know what I think? I think love is one of the greatest mysteries on earth. It's like sleep. Did you ever stop and think of sleep? You lie down in bed and you're not sleeping. All of a sudden you are asleep. Can you explain it? Well, it's just like love. The more you love people the more cruel they are to you half of the time. That's the way I think of love. And the more cruel they are the more you love them. And I think it's a mystery, what makes it.

It's like tears. Did you ever stop to think of tears and where they come from? Well, where is that fountain, where is it lodged, in the brain? Where is it? And I will tell you something more. If I were very sad, if someone close to me was about to die, I would not be able to cry, not even if you shot me. But then I go to the movie house and some kind of crazy movie—and there I cry. Well, where does the tear come from? Aw, to me it's a great mystery. And it's a foolish thing too. Like sleep....

I'll tell you a story about an Irishman that had a boy. And the Irishman didn't know a letter—but he was a wealthy farmer. And he said that his son had to go to college and that he had to be one of the most educated men in England. So fi-

126

nally he did get married and he had a son. So the son had to go to school. And he went to college. And when he was all through, he had all his degrees and he came home.

And then there was an English professor who came out and said that he would give a fortune to anyone who could beat him at history or anything that would come his way. And the Irishman said to his son, "I want you to tackle him." The son said, "I can't, Father. That's an intelligent man." "Well, that's all right, that's what I sent you to college for—to be an educated man, to be more clever than an Englishman." "Well, I can't do it." The father said, "If you don't try him then I'm going to tackle him." "Father," he said, "you can't win." "I know," he said, "but I'm going to tackle him just the same."

So they took the old Irishman into a great big dining room. I guess the table must have been 30-40 feet long. One on each end of the table. And it started this way:

The professor took one finger and he showed it to the Irishman. And the Irishman held up two. And then the professor showed him three. Aw, the Irishman was getting hot behind the collar—so he showed him his fist. So the Englishman gave a twist of his head like that, and he fished in his pocket and he brought out a beautiful apple and he rolled it to the Irishman like that. So the Irishman took it and looked at it. It was beautiful. So he put it in his pocket and he began to rake his pockets—what could he find?—all he could find was an old crust of bread. It was so hard and he was so mad, he just threw it. And the Englishman said, "Oh, my dear people, I am beaten. He's got the victory." So they took the old Irishman in triumph. They carried him all over the hall there.

And they asked the professor, "How is it that dumb fellow got the victory?"

"Oh well," he said, "he's not dumb." He said, "I showed him one finger to show him that there is one God. And he showed me two to show me there are two persons in God. So I showed him three fingers to show him there were three divine persons in God. So he showed me his fist to tell me they were all combined in one. So I rolled him an apple on the table to tell him of the temptation of Adam. So he threw me a crust of bread for the redemption of sin. That's how I was beaten."

So they asked the old fellow, how was it that he beat the professor. He said, "That fresh Englishman. I have only one eye and I know it—and he held up one finger. So I showed him two fingers to tell him I could see better with one eye than he could with two. So he showed me three fingers to say he could fight me. So I showed him my fist to show him I was ready. I'll fight him any day. So he sent me an apple to make up and be friendly. Well, all I had was an old crust of bread—and it was good enough for him."

Isn't that a nice story? I think it's a very nice story.

I guess I must tell you a story about a fox. This man, his uncle came from North Cambridge, and together they went to Trout Lake, you know, up in Cheticamp. They went out fishing for trout. They call it Cheticamp Lake, but the old people used to call it Trout Lake. I don't know how they got there. Well, it was a lie anyhow, they never went there. But he said, "When we got to the lake there, there was a fox. A beautiful fox." And my uncle said, "Don't you make a noise, now, don't you frighten the fox away. He's doing something." "What is he doing?" Well, he was lifting stones and picking worms, and then on every one of his claws he would put a worm and he would stick it out in the water. Then all of a sudden a trout would come, and he would grab it with his claws and throw it on the beach. He did that awhile. And then it didn't go fast enough. He put worms on both paws. And when he had caught maybe twenty trout—they were all big trout—his uncle said, "That's the time. You can shoot him now."

And so they shot the fox. And they had a bagful of trout and a fox. Now isn't that a beautiful story? What a nice lie. Isn't that the sweetest lie you ever heard?

You know, I was very sick one day, and I was supposed to die. I was thirteen days on the dangerous list—and Leo came in to see me. I said to him, "After I'm dead I will follow you to The Point. And you will see my soul on pebbles, on grains of sand,

129

on little pieces of straw—any place you look. I will be in front of you in fifty different shapes." And there I look. And there was Leo, crying. And I said, "Leo, I was going to tell you a story but in that case I won't tell you. You're ugly enough as you are." "Keep quiet," he said—and he was laughing through the tears.

And in the afternoon another person came and I said to them, "If you come here to cry because I'm dying, go home." And then she was laughing, she was crying—and you know, she died suddenly afterward.

And the nuns—I told them to get out of my room. They were all in there saying the rosary. But I didn't die. I wouldn't give them the satisfaction.

The Port Hood Windstorm

told by Amelia Cook

This windstorm I want to tell you about came the December before the First World War was over. It was early in the evening. And us kids were all around home. We were alone—Daddy was in Inverness—just Mama and the kids were there. And it started in.

We had like a porch on, and you could see the snow starting to swirl a little. And Mama said, "It's snowing, and I believe it's going to blow"— and just then it started blowing and boy, the wind bounced up right in a minute. And Mama said, "Well, I hope the wagonhouse won't blow down." All of a sudden the shingles started in, you know, whirling in the corner.

Mama said, "My soul, our wagonhouse is blowing down! If it doesn't come through the window, we'll be all right." And that same day we had papered the kitchen all brand new—it was coming on Christmas now. And just as Mama was walking by the window, without a word of warning, a great big rafter came right through the window and drove right clear in the front of our stove. And the wind started blowing the fire out over the floor.

And you know, a woman with four kids— poor Mama was so frightened. The glass cut her in the face and she never even noticed it. And we got an old door, an extra door on the porch, and we tried to put that over the window and put the sewing machine against that—and it was blowing across the floor. The whole bunch of us couldn't hold the door to the window.

Pat and I, we put on our coats and we ran up the field to our neighbour's house—never thinking about the wind carrying us in the woods or anything—and poor Mama never noticed. We told her, but in her excitement she never heard us. And I remember she was upstairs when we started back over with Mr. MacKinnon and his lantern. It blew so hard, my brother, it took his breath, he had to turn back. And I can hear poor Mama screeching out the upstairs window—she didn't know whether we blew away or what happened. But we managed to get there.

So our neighbour came in. He tried to get the door over the window—and the wind had begun to subside then. It only lasted about fifteen or twenty minutes. He said, "Only one thing to do is to come up and stay at our place all night." So poor Mama, she was crippled, but she could walk some. So we went and we stayed all night.

And in the morning when we came back—when we opened the kitchen door—well, I can see it yet. All the paper—see, it was newly pasted—had come down in big sheets, and the stove was solid full of snow, and the cupboard and the dishes were full of snow. And the stove so wet we couldn't start the fire. Well, talk about the time.

And in the morning when we looked around, it wasn't our wagonhouse at all, but it was our neighbour's barn—the roof had blown off. And the train came down in the night and we had noticed she stopped at our crossing—and we could see them working around, moving boards and everything. Well, that barn roof had landed right fair in the cut, on the train tracks.

And the rafter that came to us must have come oh, easy, 130 yards—and came right through the window and poked in the front of the stove.

And when we went to look around, the wire fence along the railroad was just the same as if you had taken and hung carpets on it—the hay was that thick where it blew up against it.

But our kitchen solid full of snow. We had to shovel it out. And the paper—that's what would break your heart—we'd been working at it the whole day—and what a dismal sight to go in, the paper down on top of the snow. You can look back and laugh now, but at that time you were too scared to laugh.

Max Basque Talks About Micmac Tales

My grandfather, Isaac Sack, he was visiting down at old James Paul's place, and James Paul he had a—well, it was more likely a caribou hide, because there were no deer here then—he had this bit of a moose hide, and that was his bed, near the stove. He had this old Waterloo stove, very like old William Paul at Shubie, and that was his favourite spot—there'd be room between the stove and the wall. That's where he'd sit in this spot, so he could put in the wood, now and again. There was no central heat then, and none of the houses were even finished; they were just a frame house.

Well, he said, this old gent was a-sitting by the stove, and he said, "The old lady made us all a cup of tea." Said, "We were all drinking tea, and after awhile," says, "the old lady made the rounds, another round a cup of tea." They really drank (tea), no sugar or milk. He said the old man passed out his cup, too, "Give me a little more tea," and he said the old lady just went to give him a little more tea, and she pulled the teapot away, said, "Ah, yes, Our Father's gone crazy again."

"Our Father," you know that's a great name amongst us; instead of saying "Uncle" or "The Old Man," they'd say, "Our Father." That's a little different from what we call a priest....

But the old man had squeezed his cup, you

134

could see his fingermarks all 'round. She pulled the teapot away from him, put it back on the stove. The old man just laughed, "Oh, I'll straighten it up here." He straightened it up as if it were made out of clay, and the old lady said, "That's more like it, now I'll pour you a cup of tea."

He had squeezed it up on the old lady; "Our Father's gone crazy again."

My grandfather Isaac Sack—well, that's the way it happened, he said. And some said you must have had, well, what do you call it, a hallucination, or mass-hypnosis or what. But he said, no. Grandfather said, "No, I wasn't the only one seen it, everybody seen it; just that he done so many weird things it didn't surprise nobody. Didn't surprise me any." He said just a matter of fact that things like that happened.

Like him stretching his clay pipe round his hat. He stretched his clay pipe round his hat! He'd no way to carry it, 'fraid he'd break it, so he stretched his clay pipe round his hat. That's going beyond belief. Then he straightened it up! Mass hallucination is right! Or else I suppose they'd think up who can tell the weirdest tale about old James Paul.

'Course there'd be all kind of tales, I know when I was younger, people that can remember him, and one of the other tales is this windmill somewheres near Dartmouth—this man had a windmill for grinding grain. A big windmill and had a main shaft that come right down to turn the main grindstone. And he (my grandfather Sack) said, "We was boys; we used to ride round this main shaft, like, grab it and ride round. And old James Peter Paul, he grabbed that and the whole thing stopped. And the miller come in going, 'What are you fellows doing?' And they said this old gent grabbed that pole. Miller said, 'He can't stop it, take more than the old man to do it.' The old man said, 'All I did was *this*,' and it stopped it again. The miller said, 'Don't do it any more, you've stopped the whole mill!'" Another one of those weird tales.

(*Max, I see books of Micmac stories—stories of Kluskap, Badger, things like that. And I wonder whether, when you were a child, were these stories really told to you.*) Oh, yes! Father really could tell some great stories. My grandfather, anyway, on my mother's side. I know, for instance, when we lived in Millview. Everything would be quiet, be ready to go to bed. Over at Grandfather's place. And somebody'd say—well, it's a signal for somebody to tell a story. *Ke'skw a.* Everything just went quiet. *Ke'skw a.* That means that somebody would tell a story. And Grandfather would tell—I wish to goodness I'd marked some of them down, or remembered. All the weird stories about the Badger and about the Rabbit. And even about the Frog and the Wild Geese. About the Wild Geese and the Turtle.

How the Turtle got in friends with the Wild Geese, a couple of the younger Wild Geese. He said he'd like to go south, too. He said, "Where the sun's shining all year round." Said, "We'll take you down." So they started taking him. He said, "If we get a stick, could you hang onto that stick. We'll fly south, and you hang onto the stick with your mouth. We'll take you down south." And, stories like that....

And about how there's a name for a bird when it flies, and kind of glides a bit. And how these two Geese, doing the same thing. And finally the Turtle, he had to say something. And he opened his mouth, and luckily he fell in a pond! And these two young Geese told their leader about it. He said, "Our little friend dropped down." Oh, a long story how the leader gave them particular old dickens for bringing anything with them. "Now," he said, "we'll have to go back and pick him up. Or find out how he made out." So they came back and settled on this lake.

Oh, stories like that. God! I can remember some of them, but I could never begin to tell that the way he used to tell them. He'd make that story last all evening, till we'd go to sleep, me and my brothers.... Or sometimes, when he'd see we were getting too sleepy—"I will tell you about it next time we get sleepy," or "next time we turn in." There's a lot more to that story. And then I don't know whether it's a real story he thinks up. All the weird happenings. Some of the great stories.

And about Kluskap. I guess most of it was all damn lies. I guess Kluskap was quite a smart man. But I've often heard my grandfather, he'd tell us not to believe all those foolish stories about Kluskap...about Five Islands and all that. He said, "The French made them up."

It was only when I read this—Jesuit priests—Jesuit missionaries—when they first came over, tried to convert the Micmac. They had to write to headquarters in French. He said, "The Micmacs are the hardest people to convert to Christianity. Each time we tell them anything about Jesus—they had a teacher whose teaching was so much like Jesus' teaching. And he did miracles like Jesus did. And brought the dead back to life. And made the blind see, and all that." He said, "Almost the same as the teachings of Jesus."

So headquarters in France told them to make a liar out of Kluskap. Tell them it was all fairy tales and that nobody can do that. And so they added more on to what Kluskap used to teach. Finally got to a point where the Micmac word for a real good liar: *Keluskapewin*. "You're like a Kluskap," or "You look like Kluskap." That means you're telling lies. *Keluskapewit*. "He's a liar." "He looks like Kluskap," or "He talks like Kluskap." It was a priest that (did that). He went out and Christianized the Micmac. They say that Jesus was the only teacher that taught anything like that or could do anything like that. Not Kluskap.

But, too bad they didn't find out originally just what kind of a man Kluskap was. Must be something like Zoroaster....

And then, all the strange tales about the Cold, as if it would be something like a Jack Frost. How this person was in a wigwam, how he got so cold—even his fire wouldn't burn right. And this Cold, in sort of a human form, would come to the door, and keep looking in, looking in. He knew that if his fire ever went out, that he'd come in, and that he'd freeze to death. But oh, that story's—long, long tale about this, how he got the best of—how he kept (out)—well, I'd call him Jack Frost. (**Ruth Whitehead:** *What is he called in Micmac?*) *Tkey*. Just another word for cold. *Tkey ne'apa'sit Ka'qniktuk*. The Cold was peeking in the door. Ah, I forgot—*Kimamit, Kimamit*—peeking. *Ketu' mnaqnewa'lit*. He was peeking to see if I was getting any weaker. I was getting colder.... Oh, a long tale. All evening's tale about how he got the best of that Cold, kept the Cold from coming in.

And even about Thunder, that he was around in human forms. Yes, about Thunder. *Wetiwajijik*. Our ancestors, rolling stones, or rolling logs. And how they'd get so mad. A sharp, sharp crack. *Anko'te'n. Anko'te'n*. "Watch out! Watch out!" He's getting handier. That's when the old ladies would say their prayers. Ask for some other help from somebody else—some other god form—not to let them come any nearer. And then it'd say, they'd make up a story—how this here lightning bolt was meant for them. Just happened that it turned to the right spirit. It hit a tree over there. And of course, the slivers from a tree that was blasted by

139

lightning would be the greatest thing for curing toothache and all that. Kind of weird beliefs....

And people believe, if you believe in anything strong enough. Like people believe in miracles. Well, sure enough, miracles happen to them. Something like Ste. Anne de Beaupré. John Maloney, well, he was a veteran of the First War. Me and John heard about it—they went by train. "It wouldn't do us any good because we don't believe in that. But if you believe in anything," he said, "very likely it could cure you." And it does cure you.... Power of the human mind....

Oh, tales. I often—no wonder they could tell stories, because there was no radio, no gramophone, or no nothing in the evenings, when it got dark. Might keep the home fires, keep the bonfire going, inside a camp. If it was outside, good enough—outside. Sitting all around it. And there would be nobody say anything. And then somebody would say, *"Ke'skw a. Ke'skw a."*

The Bolt of Cloth— a Pioneer Story

told by Stephen W. MacNeil

I was trying to tell the hardships the first settlers suffered and did in this country, you know, how they stuck it out and lived here. In the wilderness with nothing much to live on.

There's a story regarding that, regarding this man that found the Glengarry Mineral Spring. My grandfather, MacIsaacs, they lived down here; you can see them from the main road. That's where they landed and that's where they lived.

Well, this man, MacIntyre, came from Scotland afterwards and all the land was taken up, but he went right back there, about seven miles (inland) from here, right out to the Mineral Spring.

And it seems this fall that the potatoes failed for everybody. There was a blight or something struck and killed the crops and there wasn't too much for them to eat more than hemp, I guess.

Well anyway, his wife was a weaver from Scotland. She weaved cloth. And she weaved what they call a bolt—forty yards, you know—and she weaved that and he tied it on his back and he started in and he stopped at my great-grandfather's—on his way to North Sydney to sell this warp of cloth for to get something to eat.

And so he went to North Sydney. And it was

141

a late fall and the freeze-up was after coming in, and all this cloth that was weaved by the first settlers around here went to Newfoundland to make clothes for fishermen, you know. And when he got to North Sydney, the freeze-up came and there was no travel, no way of sending the stuff to Newfoundland.

He couldn't sell it, couldn't get a nickel for it. Had to walk back to my grandfather's place down here and not a bite to eat, only they kept him while he was there, I guess.

But he told my grandfather or told them all, I guess, to go out and tell his wife—take something with them, too, I guess (to feed them)—that he was going to Arichat the next day. It was an open port then, Arichat—it wouldn't freeze up—and he thought that there'd be a possibility of selling the cloth in Arichat.

So my grandfather went out and told MacIntyre's wife the story.

Well anyway, MacIntyre walked to Arichat.

When he got to Arichat, same story verbatim: he couldn't sell it, couldn't give it away.

So he walked back and went to my grandfather's place down there.

And my grandfather's brother was after coming in—and he was working in Halifax at something—and he came home during while all this was going on, you know. I guess he came home for Christmas, that he'd be home for Christmas, the young fellow. My grandfather then would be only about sixteen when he was travelling back and forth.

So he pitied the old fellow, he pitied MacIntyre. And he had a little money and he bought the cloth, bought this roll from MacIntyre there, and MacIntyre was happy as a clam.

He told my grandfather to go out again and tell his wife that he was going to North Sydney again. 'Course he went with the money this time, and got fifty pounds of meal, flour, whatever made it up of fifty pounds of something to eat, anyway. Tied it on his back and came back there with it and a bottle of gin.

And the next day he went home.

Gladys Ross: How I Got My Nickname

Apart from being a curious person, especially about nature and life in general, I never gave up on something that bothered me. So that beautiful spring morning while looking out the front door across the pond, I spied an unfamiliar object shining in the sun. It was the period in our history when space travel and moon walks were a household subject.

I said to myself "Maybe...," and as my husband was asleep, I decided to investigate.

Our home was built about seventy feet from a steep hill at the back and it was the only way to get to the pasture. I climbed the hill dressed in what my husband called my "pit clothes," everything two sizes too big. I called them "just outmoded" and he would tell me, "You always dress for the occasion." I still have clothes from the 'Forties!

I crawled under barbed wire and walked down a cow path. Ducking between the little hills, I could see the spot where the object lay on the side of the hill that faced my front door. I stood and stared down at a gorgeous blue rock. It was as big as a twelve-pack, rounded on each side with craters all over it, just like a moonstone.

Excited, I tried to lift it but it was impossible, yet I was determined to take it home. I started to roll it over the hilly field, up and down most of the time, on my knees. I got it under the barbed wire and finally it lay next to my veranda.

I walked in the front door and by this time my husband was puttering around the kitchen, probably watching my antics from the window. Nothing was said for a moment or two. He sure could make you squirm. By this time, I was feeling ridiculous in my get-up. Then he said with a smile, "What have you been up to now? I see you're all dressed up for a special occasion."

I blurted out, "I found the most beautiful stone in the field, it wasn't there yesterday."

Calm as a cow chewing its cud, he never seemed to hear me. I was getting exasperated. It seemed like a scene from an "I Love Lucy" show. He was enjoying my discomfort.

Lighting a cigarette, he took a few puffs and finally sauntered out to the end of the veranda. He looked down at that blue sapphire stone and said, "You just snitched the cow's salt lick."

"I never heard of such a thing!" I almost screamed. "Do you mean to tell me that beautiful stone belongs to the cows?"

"Well," he said, "if you don't believe me, take a lick." He turned to go back inside.

"Aren't you going to help me take it back?" I asked.

"What?" he said, "and be charged as an accessory?"

Well, at that moment I wished I had evolved as a snail and let the beautiful sea soothe my injured pride!

But the worst was yet to come. It meant going back uphill with the stone. After much puffing and grunting, I returned it with envy and regret.

My husband didn't waste time, telling my family and friends about the moonstone that fell out of the sky. I took the kidding for a long time with a grain of salt. But my husband never did let me forget it. He nicknamed me "Sapphire."

When Paddy Foresaw His Own Death

told by Archie Neil Chisholm

I'll give you an experience that happened probably in the middle '20s. And this is a peculiar forerunner of a person foreseeing their own death. And it starts on a Sunday afternoon when Danny Mike and Paddy were coming up from a wedding. The wedding was down in Cheticamp and they were both, to quote Danny Mike, they were both a little bit hung over coming home. It was in the horse-and-buggy days, and when they came to Terre Noire, coming down the hill at Terre Noire just before they came to a little place there's a sort of cove there and a look-off you can go down there, Paddy said to Danny, "What crowd am I seeing on the coast there?" And Danny laughed. He looked and he couldn't see a thing and he said to Paddy, "You didn't get over the wedding yet, you're still about half-cut." But Paddy says, "No, I'm seeing the..." and he says, "Danny, I want to tell you something, you're taking a body in off the rocks."

Well, Danny couldn't see a thing and he was looking carefully and he just didn't pay any attention. He dropped Paddy off at his home and he went home and he thought no more of it.

About three weeks afterwards on the morning of Halloween's Eve, Paddy and a fellow by the name of Tommy took what we call a motor boat or gasoline boat from Margaree Harbour and they went down for a load of salt to Cheticamp. After they got their load of salt they decided that they were going to hit Cheticamp. But (leaving), they were warned not to go to sea with their boat because a southeaster was coming up. You'll have to be acquainted with Cheticamp to know the *suête*. Two hours before a southeaster hits the people of Cheticamp will know it's coming. It's called a *suête*.

So they were warned not to go out to sea. And one of them jokingly said to the fellow that warned him, "We're going out to sea. We'll make Margaree Harbour or hell, one or the other, before the evening." So they went out with their load. And salt is a rather treacherous load, anyway. As they were only out to sea about a half hour when they realized that the warning should have been well taken because the southeaster hit. And now they were in a position where they could not come back in because of the rocky coastline and they had to head for Margaree Harbour. Now, remember, they were both young, powerful, and expert in a boat and they figured they'd make it.

When the storm hit, this began to trouble the people in Cheticamp, and they began to call up. The phone was quite in use then, and they'd call up the people at Grand Etang and Point Cross and St. Joseph du Moine wondering if they could see a sign of this boat on the coast. An awful lot of the people went down to the shoreline, and occasionally they could hear the sound of the boat. As she'd come up on the crest of the wave they'd hear the putt of the motor, and then she'd go down in the trough of the wave again. After about probably an hour everybody from Margaree Harbour down knew that these people were at sea and the deadly danger they were in but they couldn't send anything out to try to get them because they'd only lose their own lives.

But strange as it seems they made right up as far as right off the shore at Belle Côte, right off that cove. And there was a crowd on the shore and they could hear the boat. Then finally they lost sight or sound of the boat and they knew that she went down. Now that evening Tommy's body was found and it was carried in from the rocks.

Now, you'd think that was the end of the story but it's not. Danny Mike—there was about three days afterwards, he was coming up in the same place with the same horse-and-buggy coming home—he'd been to some business—and they still hadn't found Paddy's body. And as Danny was (coming to) the same spot, this time he saw the crowd that was there. There was a huge crowd down on the shore and as he was coming close, he saw them taking the body off the rocks. This time it was Paddy's body. And he realized at that time that only three weeks prior to that Paddy had seen the forerunner of his own death! Now, that's not a make-up story. That's true.

Percy Peters and the Wild Cow

Well, it's about a cross cow I bought. And, it was the day the Canso Causeway opened. And I left here in the morning with the truck, and I went up through the North Side of East Bay. I picked up a couple of calves and I picked a cow or two up. And I went on into Eskasoni, the reservation.

And there was a fellow there who looked after the cattle and the horses for the reservation. I got acquainted with this man—Victor Jeddore was his name.... And anything was around for sale, he'd always tell me when I'd be going through, and I'd pick it up.

So, I went out this morning—Saturday morning—and I met him. He said, "Peter, there's a cow up in Castle Bay for you there. At Alex MacDonald's. He told me when I see you to tell you to come." So I said, "Well, I'll go right up." He said, "I'll go with you." I said, "Yes, I would like your company very well...."

So anyway, we went along, went up—drove down to his house. He was a bachelor, by the way, this MacDonald. And of course, being around with the cattle, just himself, they got domesticated. So this particular cow didn't like a stranger. But I wasn't aware of that, getting there.

So I knew him, and I said, "Do you have a cow for sale, Alex?" "Yes." I said, "Well, we'll go up

149

and have a look at her." He said, "You fellows stay out on the road, and you walk up the road a way. Don't come in the field—she'll be up in the pasture." He didn't say why.

So we walked up the road. And the cow was over with the other ones. She came to him all right. But she was watching us, walking up. She didn't pay any attention to him. And I saw her tail switching back and forth, back and forth. I said to Victor, I said, "You know, that cow looks like she could be pretty wiry. She's watching us—she doesn't like strangers." "Yes," he said, "I think that's right, too."

So anyway, he got her by the head—he never took her by the horns—and she walked over so far. So I was going to get through the fence and go in and have a look at her, see her condition. "Oh," he said, "you stay out there now. If you can see her well enough from there." "Yes," I said, "that's all right."

So, I looked at her, and I figured what was in her, and she was fat. And I said, "That's all right. What do you want for her?" And he told me. And I said, "Well, that's fine. You take her to the barn and I'll buy her." "Yes. But you stay out there." So we walked down the road back to the house. And he put her in the barn.

Alex came back. He said, "Now you give me your rope, Peters, and I'll put her on the truck for you." That's fine, sure. "She'll follow me anywhere." So, she did. But once she got on the truck, she started to raise old Cain with strange cattle. And she was confined, and that's something she was never used to. Of course, I suppose strangers, too, we upset her some. She was wiry, starting.

So anyway, I got ahead of the story. When up in the field he had ahold of her, he put his arm around her head, and he put the arms around and he blindfolded her. And Victor said to me, "Peters, there's something wrong with that cow—he makes her blind." He blindfolded her. I said, "Well, yes." But I didn't think like that.

So anyway, loaded her, and I came home. And I told my son, I said, "Look, that cow is on there. There's three of them. But the one who's in the middle, I think she's rough. I don't know what's wrong."

My gracious, we found out she started to go for us. And so I put another rope on her, and we tied her into the barn, paid off the slack off the truck. We locked her in the stanchion there.

So, my son had killed some cattle in the morning, and then we had to bone some beef, and we finished that. So about half past two or so I said, "Well, we'll water up the cattle. Probably it'd be a good idea to put her out on tether, and let her thick up. It'll be over the weekend before we'd be hanging up."

So anyway. By gracious when we got her outside, mister, she was woolly and rough. She started for us. Well we had to keep out of her way. She was really, really treacherous. She made a run for us, and we jumped her. I should have had the second rope on her. And we tried to get her on the bar. But the truck was still there, so I lashed her up to the truck. I had a cattle truck. And I tied onto the frame. And she had a long rope on her. And jesus, start—oh, was she wild! She went around the front of the truck, around the back of the truck. And she saw me—what I was trying to do, gather some more slack in and tie her up shorter so could get her back in. But it didn't work like that. She saw me, and then she tried to get in under the truck after me. Oh, she was roaring!

Anyway. She made a jump around the front of the truck and then she tried—she beat the grill in—a big Mercury front. She had a big round grill on them then. And she beat that all in with her horns, her head. She'd stand off and she'd belt that. So. Then she changed her mind; she went around the truck again. She snapped the rope. And left about eight feet on it. She took off.

She went down in the field, in the corner down there I was showing you. And there was an old car body there, a fellow left there. Right at the line fence. And by gracious, we got her locked in behind there. Bob took the truck and crowded her in behind. So I was sneaking in behind the old car body, trying to get ahold of the rope and walk out to the truck and fasten her up again. Oh, my God, the old car upholstering was full of hornets. Well I had to get out of that. I don't know if the cow got any on her, but that didn't help any.

152

And when she came out again, she took another whack at the truck. And then she came up the field. And the cattle were here—the other ones I had in the pen there—they were scared to death of her. She started then. She hooked one and then hooked the other, drive them away. And then she took right for us. And I've—"Gosh," I said. She took off. She smashed the fence in between the neighbours, and they had cattle. And those cattle knew there was something wrong. By gosh, she took after them. And they scattered.

So, the young fellow's father there, he ran—he seen her coming. I hollered at him, "Get out of her way!" I said, "She'll go at you!" I knew she would. Well, he grabbed a piece of two-by-three, and he was going to confront her with this. But boy, she'd have none of that—she took after him. Well he just threw that and then took off. And...it landed in front of her and she struck it with her horns and drove it right over her back. You know, hit it with her horns.

Well, she went in through their cattle, and she went around. And he tried to head her off. And I was hollering at him, "Get away from her. Don't bother with her. Someone's going to get hurt." So then I thought of it. It was that time of year, you couldn't use a gun, you know—you couldn't go in the woods with one. So I ran to the phone and I called the Mounted Police, and I told them that I had a cross cow got away on me, and I wanted to get her before she hurt somebody, and I have to have permission to use some rifles. And I said, "She's cross." He said, "Are you sure it isn't a bull?" "Well now," I said, "I'm not trying to be funny or saucy with you, but I know a bull from a cow. And I know a cross one from a quiet one. I've got a cross cow, and there's people picks blueberries, and if she confronts them, she'll hurt somebody. So he told me, "Take them."

So my gracious, she was on the way. She went over there, and the old fellow tried to stop her. And she went after him. And he just got through the fence in time, and she was right behind him. And he jumped in through the pole fence again, got back in. And then she took off out the wood road.

Well, we didn't know—you couldn't trust her. She'd waylay you on the road. She'd hide in the bushes and if she heard you coming, she'd come right after you. She wouldn't run away from you at any time. So anyway—I tried to shorten it up as much as I can, but I tell all the detail as I remember it.

We got some guns, and we went down to the back there. Gracious. We heard this coming through the woods. She went down to a low place and she got a drink of water. And boy, she was coming up this wood road on the run, coming as hard as she could come. And she saw us. And boy, she was looking just.... And we jumped back and hid in the woods. Three of us—my son Bob, and my wife's brother, Jim Jollimore. My gracious, she got looking. We could see her. She was looking to see where we were; she wanted to get another crack at us. Oh, she was like that.

Anyway, we followed her. Then she went down across a barren away out the back there, and we lost track of her. So we followed around from dark. But you had to be cautious. You didn't know where she'd waylay you. She'd waylay in the woods and then come out at you.

Anyway, we hunted until just at dark—dusk. I came around a turn in the road and there she was. She had been feeding—there was some green stuff around some old birches—little birch switches. And she began to feed there. And the long piece of rope—she was reaching around for grass. And she tangled herself; she wound around, turn after the other—she wound herself up, and she was there standing with her head down.

Well, it was too dark, from the distance we were, to take a shot at her and miss her. And I didn't want to ruin any meat. No good shooting them through the body. Anyway, I said, "We'll just leave her. She may be wound up enough and not go back the other way and unwind herself. She'll be there in the morning and we'll get her. It'll be Sunday morning."

So by gracious, we went out bright and early: she was gone. She got herself clear. Well, which way she went—the ground was hard, you couldn't see any hoofprint. So we went down on a little bar-

155

ren and we saw some impression where she'd gone through this barren. I said, "Now I know, she's gone to the brook. There's a brook there. She's gone for a drink."

Well, we didn't find her. Well, we hunted Sunday, we didn't find her. And then finished our work Monday, and we took off again. We didn't find her.

And Tuesday went down. And I said, "She's hanging around the brook there somewhere. And she's going to hang around where there's water." There was a marsh there. "And she'll be wherever there's any feed." See, there'd be some green feed then. In July. What day was it? Was it in July the Canso Causeway opened? I thought it was August or July. It doesn't matter. Anyway, I know it was—that's the day.

And so I said—we had dinner here. I said, "I'm going to head down where I think this cow is hanging out." So we walked down after, and we went down in the back here to the brook. Big brook—that's the big brook that goes through the city and causes all the trouble. The Wash Brook, they call it. You've heard of it, probably. Go down by the City Hospital. Well that runs from all the way in back there. Several lakes, and big barrens.

Anyway. By gracious, we went about 200 feet in towards the brook and we heard this crashing. We were talking, of course, and she heard our voices, and out she come. And of course, we were on a bit of a path, and we jumped and sidestepped her, and she went by us. But she was looking.

In the meantime, my brother Bill was home from Halifax. He went out that way, from another farm up the road there, on horseback. And he had a rifle. And when she got by us, she took off. We watched the direction. She was on the run, too. And her head going, looking, looking, looking, to see where we were. She was—looking for prey.

So anyway, we hollered to him as hard as we could. Wind was favourable and he could get it in the wind direction. "She's heading your way! Watch her!" My gracious, she broke out in the field on the next farm. And she momentarily stopped. And he fired. He struck her right on the end of the horn. And he kind of grazed her. But she kind of tumbled, so she picked up her feet again. And she went over to the other line fence and she crashed that.

So, there was a bit of blood came off of the pith of the horn—there wasn't nothing. We went over—he showed us where he fired. When we got over, oh, just a little lick and spit of blood here, on a leaf, and a little on a fern. And then there'd be a long ways before— Well, we tracked her all afternoon. And couldn't get her. The further she went, the less blood was coming. It was only superficial, you know.

Anyway. We went up, away up in the woods. And then it clouded over and it began to shower a little, just light. So I smoked at that time. We stopped and took a package of cigarettes and had a smoke. And my son and his uncle were down on the wood road, not too far from us. We had to keep everybody in line to know where they were: if you had to fire, you wouldn't shoot somebody.

So anyway, we were standing there talking. I stood my rifle against a tree and he stood his. Puffing on a cigarette. And by gracious, I thought I seen something moving up in the clearings, in the hardwood: a big white spruce, about so size. Here she was standing directly behind that. And every once in awhile she'd peek the head out behind, watching for us. I said, "Gosh, Bill, look at her looking." So I reached for the rifle. And I took a shot. And I hit her right on the peen of the head. Right here in the high skull. Down she went. Bill said, "You got her."

Well, the words were no sooner out of our mouth, when up she come, and she headed down for us! We didn't have too much cover. My gracious, she made her right for us. We ducked in a bunch of little bushes and stayed quiet. I was trying to get a bead on her. I wanted to get a head shot and put her down. But she veered off.... And she didn't come twenty feet from my son and his uncle, sitting down on the road—they were making a cigarette. And she jumped pretty near over them—well, the noise, you know. "Well," he said, "she's gone this way."

Well, we saw no more of her then. We hunted all through the week, every chance we'd get. So I went out the road to pick up—a lot of cattle around that time—so I went out to pick up some calves the following Saturday. That's the last we'd seen of her, that evening. And when I came home she said, "You know, that cow just broke out of the woods and came in here with the other cattle." So a fellow left a rifle here with a scope sight on it, you know. So I picked it up. And I seen her, she was coming up the field. Well, I told her to call the rest of the boys that were here, trying to get a shot at her. And I said, "I'll go down back with the 12." I took the 12 and a rifle slug. I went down around and I got in behind her. And she came up. And the other cattle knew it was her, and they were scared of her. They kept away. She was crazy. She'd go right in amongst them and put the horns to them.

Anyway. They came up in the field there. And I broke out through the woods and I come to the field. And I got behind a little clump of alder. And boy, she only come up, and she was galloping—oh, crazy! She hadn't stopped. Anyway, I was crouched down. And she turned, and she come right directly. And it just seemed to me like she was looking, like she knew where I was. But I don't think she did. But to me, she did. And the head was going from side to side. And she was—oh, she had a determined fight in her face. So by gracious, she was getting handy. And I said, "By jumping, I've got to do something!" I said to myself, "I don't know what to do. If I miss her, and she comes at me, if she sees me, I have no way to get away."

So I kept, got a bead on her, and I fired. And boy, I seen something flying out the other side of

159

her. Well, I shot her right through the corner of the mouth and cut the tongue off—the bullet. The tongue went flying across the field. Anyway, that's a kind of a shame—I couldn't help it. I tried to get her in the side of the head—that's my purpose of firing at the head.

And anyway, she turned and come up the field. And she got in amongst the cattle. And I could see the blood on the white side of her face. I didn't hit her where it was vital at all. But anyway she came up, and they tried to get a shot. And you had to be careful where we were shooting—she was on the gallop, so you had to be careful.

Anyway, my brother was home that Saturday, and he came up across the field there. So he was going to try to head her back. And I hollered, "Don't get in her way—she'll get right onto you." And she would, too. And by gracious, he didn't leave a time enough, and by gracious, she took after him. And he turned to run, and she got him right in the rear end on her horns and just lifted him right up in the air—threw him up in the air. When he came down, she struck him in the back of the head, here, with the horns—right in behind the ear. And then she tried to jump on him.

Well I ran, and I had the gun ready, to distract her from him, 'cause she was going to jump on him. And she came after me. Well then her attention was drawn to another fellow. She went over after him. Well, you had to be careful how you shot—somebody'd get shot, you know.

So anyway. My son got a shot at her, hit her right in the side of the horn close to the head. Well that kind of put her off balance a little and she got a little bewildered, and she went in circles....

I suppose you think it was poor shooting, but she was on the run. It's hard enough to shoot one standing. Anyway, I don't know who else it was. I think it was my brother Bill or Bob, my son, got the last shot on her, and put her down. I went up and bled her, and that finished her.

When Trueman Clark Went Overboard

Oh, that's before I went in the army. Yeah, that was the *Lord Strathcona*, I was onto her. I went to Montreal, I guess, and then back to Sydney, and started across (the Atlantic). And out off of Cape Race—about halfway across to Ireland, pretty near, and struck a storm there. I was on watch, then, from eight to twelve, I guess it was.

Half past eleven, I started aft with the tea-kettle, to call the watch. And when I got down to the midship there—a little more (near the) engineer's quarters there. Sea struck me and put me overboard. And I could see the old boat going along—I was looking at the lights up there, at her side, the lights. The first thing she rolled down again, and came over towards me. And when she rolled down, the water went in over the side—I went in with it. Another—oh, I suppose another ten or twelve foot, I'd have been out underneath the stern and gone.

I went and called the watch and went back up and back down. Never bothered me. I remember I kept on going just the same.

There was over I went on another one. Some fellow said, "If it'd been me, when I got back aboard—when I got my feet on the land—I'd of never went off it again." So I don't know how he'd have got home, if he had of! He either had to come by water or go by air. (Trueman laughs.)

(*Let me understand. You were walking along with a teakettle in your hand.*) Yes. (*And the sea came in.*) Sea came and struck me and put me right overboard. (*What did you think?*) What did I think? I didn't think of nothing. I was thinking whether I was going to go in underneath the stern or not—that was the most that was in my mind. But I could see the lights and all. But when I came in over the side and I went to go out again, I guess under the ladder going up on the poop aft, the poop—I gripped that with my hand and I held on. And I still had the kettle in the other hand—I never let go of it when I went overboard! (*You never lost your kettle!*) No, no.

(Did everybody believe you when you said you were washed over and washed back on?) What in the hell could they do?...

162

Rita Joe Tells the Legend of Mud-Lane

Once upon a time many moons in the past, there lived a King in a foreign country, with three daughters who loved him very much. Their way of expressing love would always be, the first daughter would say, "Father, I love you, more than all of the money in the world," the second daughter would say, "Father, I love you, more than all of the finest silk in the world," the youngest daughter would say, "Father, I love you, more than all of the pork and strawberries in the world," because truthfully that is what she loved to eat most in the world.

The King must have been cruel and vain, because he did not like the way Mud-lane expressed herself. He wanted to be loved more than all of the finest riches in the world.

He told the guards, "Take that girl out of my sight and chop off her hands, hang her on a tree until she blows away like dust." There she hung tied on a tree waiting for death, her grieving heart inconsolable because of the cruelty of her father. When she could cry no more, she sang, her mournful cry heard only by animals and birds of the forest.

> *I loved him more than words can say,*
> *I loved him, only my way,*
> *It was not enough, it was not enough,*
> *Oh my, oh my I say*
> *I am dead.*

A young prince from another country happened to be passing by riding on horseback. He heard the grieving song, so sad but beautiful. He searched the area until he found her, but when he tried to untie her she cried:

I loved him more than words can say,
I loved him only my way,
It was not enough, it was not enough,
Oh my, oh my I say
I want to die.

He loosened the bonds, took her down gently and took her home to his queen mother in the castle, curing the stumps that were hands before.

Mud-lane wanted to die, feeling useless without hands. The prince told her that she was the most beautiful person that he ever knew, her songs made him happy, her presence made the castle a happy home. The queen loved her like a daughter she never had. Mud-lane agreed to stay.

Then the prince had to travel to another country, to do service for his queen mother. That is the time he realized that he did not like to be away from Mud-lane. The longer he stayed away the more love he felt for the girl with no hands. When he returned home, he asked Mud-lane to be his wife. The queen mother gave her blessing.

Now Mud-lane knew much happiness, being loved by the prince and his mother. She sang the songs of happiness.

I love him more than words can say
I love him only my way,

164

It is enough, it is enough,
Oh my, oh my I say
I am loved.

Then the prince had to go away again to another country, and knowing that Mud-lane was expecting their first-born, his thoughts were of a happier future.

The prince stayed in the foreign country longer than expected. The queen mother looked after Mud-lane. Then it was time for her to have the child. The birth turned out to be twin boys. That made the queen mother so happy that she sent a messenger to the prince, stating that Mud-lane and twin boys were well.

The messenger rode far and fast trying to get the message to the prince, but he got tired nearing night, he stopped at an inn by the wayside hoping to rest and go on. But they put a sleeping potion in his drink that put him into a deep slumber. The innkeeper found the message in his pocket, but instead of the happiness relayed in the message he changed it to say that the twins were ugly and half *jooge-gij* (snake) and the queen mother hated them.

The prince received the message. He was sad but promised to love Mud-lane and the twins as well. The same thing happened again to the messenger at the inn on his way back, and the return message was full of hate.

When Mud-lane read the message of hate, she took a few clothes and the twins and went deep into the wood, making a promise to herself that no one would ever hurt her or her children again.

She walked a great distance. Becoming thirsty and looking for water, she came to a *Si-boo* (river). She put one child in one pocket and the other one in another pocket. Then stooping over she tried to drink. One twin began to slip out of her pocket. Mud-lane reached out with the stump of her hand to grab the child and her hand became whole. Then from the other pocket another twin fell out. She reached out with the other stump and that too became whole. She did not understand what had happened, but she was happy because then the children would get better care.

She found an old cabin in the wood and cleaned it, making a home for herself and the children. With time they became contented with not a worry in the world.

When the prince returned home and heard all that had happened he was angry. The palace guards arrested the innkeeper and got the whole story. He was punished.

The queen mother wanted her grandchildren returned. She cried every day but nobody heard of them. The prince looked far and wide wanting to see his precious children, and with a heavy heart he searched for his lost love. When there was no place else to search he walked into the deep wood with wishes in his heart to see the two boys. He saw the cabin with two small boys playing outside. Not having seen them before he hopefully asked,

"Where is your mother?" They replied, "Near the river." Then he asked, "What is her name?" In unison they replied, "Mud-lane!" Then he gathered them in his arms and ran to the river where Mud-lane was washing their few clothes.

When she saw her prince husband, she held out her beautiful hands, the hands that all of his Kingdom were to know with her love and beauty.

I love her more than words can say
I love her only my way,
It is enough, it is enough,
Oh my, oh my I say
Mud-lane is my love.

George Rambeau's Forerunner

(*Did you ever see anything...?*) Well, I saw something once. But...I couldn't know and I didn't know.

An old gentleman down here—Briand—died. And he was a nice old fellow, and we all liked him, you know. So there was me and me brother—we were two young fellows—and a first cousin of ours. We were down to the wake. He was wakin' home in his own house. It was just about sundown—nice fine evening.

And when we got down to where he was living, we saw three women coming from the way of the house, coming towards us. There was a fence at that time along the road. And they were on the inside of the fence, on the field side. But they were coming right along the fence, pretty close to us. We didn't know who they were. They looked like strangers to us. We never saw—we knew every woman 'round from White Point to South Harbour, but we knew we never saw them before. Or we didn't think we did.

But when they were getting up pretty close. there was one of them looked to me like Paddy Dunphy's wife—the one we were talking about there? Helen Jane Curtis's mother? And I knew her as well as I knew meself. I had it in mind to speak to her when she came abreast, you know?

Just before they came abreast of us, they turned, away from us. And they walked away from us, and there was a path going from the house down to the shore. They walked over till they struck that path, and they turned down on it, went down a little piece. And they started—they were kind of on their hunkers—you'd think they were picking berries or some flowers or something.

So I went to the house. We went right to the house, and there was a woman there. And I asked her what three women were here. She said there were no three women there. The only women were there was Mrs. Dunphy, John Dunphy's wife, and Paddy Dunphy's wife was there—but they had gone home around noon time. That was all right. It bothered me, I....

Next morning, we had to take him to Dingwall to bury him in the boat. So we put the casket on a barrow, and we were carrying him to the shore—poles, you know, on our shoulder. And when we came to this place, we laid him down to have a rest. There weren't too many of us. So this young fellow that was with me and me brother, when we laid him down, he came over to me and he said, "This is where these three women were picking the flowers last evening." Be God, it struck me right in the mind that that's where we stopped with him. The image of them never went out of me mind. I could picture them—they all wore the same clothes. Big women.

About a week after I went to his daughter— she lived there—went to the house. And I told her the story. She said, "Would you know the women, do you think, if you saw them?" "Yes," I said, "if I ever saw them, I'd know them." She went and brought a picture to me, with three women on it: Briand's three sisters. There they were, boy, with just the same clothes on as—everything just exactly the same as we saw them.

(*And where were they at the time?*) Down in St. Pierre and Miquelon. (*Not in Cape Breton at all?*) No. All three of them were down in St. Pierre. That's where Briand belonged to....

(*So what did that make you think?*) That's the only thing about that. If they'd have kept on coming a little farther, I'd have spoke. And maybe I wouldn't have been able to speak, I don't know. But if they had of kept on coming and I spoke, I'd have maybe learnt more. But 'twasn't to be that way. I wasn't to speak, nor they weren't to keep on comin' to us. (*Instead they turned....*) They turned away. Before they got to us they turned away, and went down to the path that we carried him down to the shore on, and stopped. Now that was just about sundown I'd say. The sun wasn't down, but it was pretty close to it. Nice evening.

The S & L Railroad Got Through Snow
told by Doug MacCormick

Wintertime, first thing, those switches have to be cleaned out for trains to operate. Then your railroad crossings, you've got to salt them—so the train can travel all during the storm, freezing cold nights, so it wouldn't ice up. But if it got ahead of you, on the weekend like, and everything froze up, then you've got to dig it all by hand—an awful lot of work. You clean your switches, shovel all that out.

Then you've got to plow it, run a flanger through.

I remember leaving here on a Monday morning, leaving here in a snowstorm, go down to keep the collieries going in New Waterford—three collieries in New Waterford—keep them open, keep them going—get back home nine o'clock on a Thursday night—four days. Sleet storm. The wires came down. Couldn't get any communication from dispatching office to us, to give an order to tell us to come home—and we had to travel by train orders. Highways blocked, nobody could get down to us. And we were just flanging and plowing and digging out switches all day long—snow piling in, ice piling in, digging—and nighttime, we'd sleep in the flanger, get our meals downtown.

Some bad storms. We used to get buried in snowstorms. I remember we were coming down—Dr. Maxwell from Dominion got married, and the only way he could get to Sydney was to run a special train—a fast engine, Engine 45—and a van. They came to within a mile and a half of Sydney, when they got buried in the Banjo. They were buried there. The engine was covered. She stalled in there, stuck in there, and everything drifted over. That thing was 14-15 feet high. And they were inside the van—had some coal and taking coal out of the bunker for the engine, keep the fire going. And that was the first night of his honeymoon.

And we came from Waterford with the plow in back of him. He didn't have any plow. He wanted to catch the fast express leaving Sydney. And the company put out a train for him. The next morning Dan Gillis with a horse and sleigh went up and took them into Sydney.

Well, to get that engine and that van out of that, there was a gang of men who worked at the coal banks, dumping coal—about forty to fifty men—came with shovels and started shovelling that out. And when they got the engine out, they put us in it. We put two engines on it, you know? We put our plow ahead and we had two engines and then our flanger behind—and we made a race for it. About half a mile, as fast as that thing could go—to drive through to open it up. We'd shoveled the train out first—but there was another seventy-five feet of snow ahead of us. That train wasn't a quarter of the way through when she got stuck. We hit the bank of snow and—oh, the snow flew up, broke the glass in the engine and everything. We came at it half a mile, everything was in it, wide up, plow ahead of you—and we got through it. You had to stand on the flanger and hold on, you'd be rolling, the stoves would be tied down and everything.

And I saw times when we *didn't* get through. I saw snow at Grand Lake where the whole day, where the snow drifts across the lake onto the track there—the only way we could get through it, we shoveled, we dug holes every fifty feet— shoveled holes down with a gang of men—the men would have to put it up from one shelf (up) onto another shelf to get it out. Now when you'd get back with the engine, you'd take a run at that—

172

and when you'd hit that, the hole would give you a chance to get clear of the snow in front of you— four or five times of running at that to go the full length before we got through. Snow, my god, talk about snow!

I remember 1967, it was like cement. You couldn't go five feet—the snowplows would all go crossways on the road—snow and ice would build up and lift up and you'd go off the road. The Seaboard was pretty near out of coal. It was on a Sunday. That was the generating plant. And when they went down, the lights were going to go out. And we worked all day Saturday, Saturday night, Sunday—at last the only way we could get down, we had to get the city plow to plow the track, put a highway plow on the railway track—that would get us down to the top of the rail. Then put the picks to it. Sunday evening we got down to the Seaboard—and they had half a car of coal left when we got there. Tough, tough winters.

I remember one February, in 1933, I think, it was 23 below—I've seen 14 below, digging ice, get their hands frozen. The winter of '38, when we built Number 18 Colliery, it was cold going—men with frozen noses every day. Some fellows up there step-dancing, trying to keep themselves warm. Cold winters, boy.

And summer, I remember going down Waterford branch when the rails got tight, when they expanded with the heat, and it buckled. I used to cut the rail on the slant, on an angle—well, the two ends when I cut through went by each other fourteen inches, lapped. Then you'd have to cut the fourteen inches off and hook it up—expansion. We'd take one of those big engines with the water tank on and the engine. You'd move over the track very slowly—the main engine on one side of the kink and the tender on the other side. Then you had weight holding that track down. Then you put the man on the torch to cut the rail—nothing would move. A safe way to cut it. If you cut a rail on the bottom and you straddle it—the rail might go up in the air six feet, buckle up. If you cut it on the top, that pressure will go down to the ground. If it comes up, you'll get an awful lift, it'll kill you.

I saw in Waterford, they had a run-off wreck down there and the rails curled up underneath the derailment—and the splice bars holding the rails together were still on. And this man went to cut the rails clear, cut the splice bars off—and when he cut the last bolt they flew—hit him in the head and killed him right there....

I started out under my father. Then when he retired, I became boss of the section crew, about 1945. Then about 1952 I became assistant road-master—that's for the whole railroad. I was a company official then. Then about 1966 I became roadmaster for the whole railroad—till 1978. I worked steady fifty-one years on the railway.

Teaching the Crows a Lesson

told by Bill Daye

When I was living in South Bar, I planted a garden every year, a nice garden for myself—corn, some years. There was a big, heavy grove of tall spruce growing just out alongside, outside of the fence where the garden was planted. And there were a couple of crows, a pair of crows nesting there all the time. They had never bothered my garden or anything that I had—cherries, fruit of all kinds—they had never bothered a thing.

This year they hatched out a couple of young crows, there were two or three. I went out one morning after planting the corn. I kept an eye on it. For two or three weeks after, the corn was sprouted up through the ground, maybe two or three inches. The young crows were pulling it out. I looked up at the two fellows perched on the tree and I said, "Listen, boys—those kids are not going to play around with my garden, or they're going to pay for it. Now you'd better call them home, or that's the end of it. I'm not planting corn for them to eat."

After having a feed of lobsters, I had quite a few shells and the old bodies. I put them out where the corn was, in between the rows. I put some dead grass over it, and I covered up a big fox trap inside of that, under the grass. I went in the house.

Five minutes after, the crows were screeching, cawing, crowing, flying up and down, diving to the ground, going in circles, turning upside down in the air—raising hell. One of the little fellows had his foot in the trap. "Well," I said, "I told you fellows about this—you're going to get in trouble if you're playing with my garden."

I drove a stake in the ground and I tied the little crow by the leg to the stake, with about two yards of good, strong cord. I took out the tail feathers and I put them on the top of the stake, pointing upwards to the sky. And I said to the big fellows that were up there on the tree, I said, "Listen, any of you fellows touch my garden, you're going to get the same treatment."

So I went in the house. I left the little crow there. About an hour after, I come out, the little crow was gone. He was clever enough to pick the knots off the cord that I had tied him with, and walk into the woods. God knows how long he had to walk around, how many months before his feathers grew out again and he was able to fly.

And there was never a crow came in and bothered my garden any more. They would be around the field picking berries, perched on the fence, everywhere you could think of—but not one of them ever came and molested my garden again.

Joseph D. Sampson's Tale of Three Giants

It's a long story, and it's a story that makes sense in a way, and no sense.

(*Do you enjoy these stories?*) Oh yeah, oh yeah, yeah. But I don't tell them, because there's nobody here to tell them to, see. People don't seem to be interested any more.

I've still got it in my mind just the same, though, just the same, like they were told to me. Just learned them by going somewhere where they were telling those stories, just hearing them, picked them up word by word. They were all in French.

(*Does the story have a name?*) No, I never heard a name about it. The way it went, it was three guys, it was three giants (Brise-Montin, Brise-Bois, Brise-Fer; ...Mountain, ...Tree, ...Iron). And they were good and strong, but they wanted to build themselves stronger so they could fight their way right through the world, with nobody would bother them. They could have been the king of everything. Animals, as well as the rest. So, that's the way that it's supposed to start.

Those three guys, they were supposed to be awful strong. Well, they took a walk in the woods to try themselves how good and strong they were. So, they all were strong, but they didn't feel they were strong enough to do what they wanted to do.

177

So they came back home and they stayed home for seven years. They were supposed to be drinking at their mother, drinking milk and things like that. For seven years.

After the seven years, they went back for a walk. And then they found that they were pretty good. Well, one came back, and he went in the forge, and he got the blacksmith to make him a cane, a thousand-pound cane, walking cane, thousand pounds. So he said, "With this, we should be able to fight our way through the world."

So there was a king, and he had his girl stolen by a giant. And he had never found her. And the guy that had stolen the girl, he had put her in a hole underground, where nobody would find her. And he had three giants to look after her, and a beast they call the Seven-Headed Beast.

Well, the king put like a word outside, if there was anybody that'd find this girl and take her over to him, he would give her to them to be married—give his girl to be married. Well, that was all right.

So they started to go in the woods to try to find the girl. Being she had been stolen, they would have liked to find where she was. So they walked and walked until they found a big hole in the ground. When they found the hole in the ground, they were trying to listen in the hole. They couldn't see any bottom or anything. Tried to look and listen. They couldn't hear too much.

So, Brise-Fer told the other guys, "You go

down to that city, go downtown. Buy me a big basket, and plenty of rope." He said, "I want to go down there and find out what is in there."

So they went down, they bought a rope and a big basket, and they came up with it. Now, when they came up, he asked them, which one of them would try to go down. Well it was Brise-Montin, he said, "I'll try it, I'll go down."

So they tied a rope on the basket and jumped in, and started to go down. When he came not quite halfways, the noise was so bad, the chains and the hollering and Christ knows what, he was frightened. He came up.

So when he came up, this guy asked him what it was like there. "Oh," he said, "there is nobody can get in there. There's so much noise and so much hollering, you can't get there because you don't know what's going to happen."

So the other fellow, Brise-Bois, he said, "I'm going to go." He said, "I'll bet you I'll go now." So he took the basket, and they took the rope, and tried to slide him down. He went a little further, but he couldn't go right down to the bottom. So anyway, when he got far enough—he had a bell with him—when it was far enough, ring the bell for them to haul him up, he couldn't go any further. (*Why couldn't he go further?*) With the noise, and the racket that was in there, he was kind of scared. He didn't want to go any further.

So anyhow, they hauled him back. When he came up, it was the same thing. They asked him what was wrong down there, he said, "You can't get there. It's impossible. The noise, and the hollering, and all kinds of beasts in there. I don't know what it is. We can't get there."

So the guy that had that iron cane there—thousand-pound iron cane—Brise-Fer. He said, "I'm going to go down." He said, "If there's any way at all to reach down, I'm going to reach down." He said, "When I'll be down there, if there is something to be done, I'm going to do it. But if I happen to meet the girl, and send her up, don't forget, send for me. Send the basket down for me. Because, if I ever come back on top of the hole, you wouldn't live to tell the story."

So they had promised him to haul him back, if he had found the girl.

So he went down there, he went far down there. And they couldn't stand by the hollering, and cripes knows what's going on—chains, and cripes knows.

Anyhow, he started walking, and he passed a couple of rooms, and by-and-by came across this girl. She was there. There were two of those giants that were looking after her—they were to pass there, I think it was two or three times a day. And that Beast with Seven Heads used to pass once a day.

So when Brise-Fer saw her, he asked her if she was the girl that was stolen, king's daughter. She said, "Yes, I am. But I'm being watched by three of those giants and the Seven-Headed Beast

180

that's coming around once a day." She said, "I can't move from here. It's impossible."

"Well," he said, "you got any remarks on you, or something that your father gave you, or your mother, or any of your parents had given you?" She said, "Yes. I've got a handkerchief that my father gave me, with a golden apple and a silver apple and *pomme d'alliance*—a remembering apple, something to remember...." They were printed on the handkerchief.

(*An apple of remembrance?*) That's more like it. She said, "That's a gift my father gave me." So he said, "Will you be kind enough to give it to me, in case that I'll be able to pass you over, pass you up?" So, she gave it to him.

And when he got through talking with her, there were three guys came around. So he just happened to lift his cane and hit them. So, he killed them.

So he went as far as the hole with her, and he put her in the basket, and he rang the bell for them to haul her up, to haul her up on deck. When they got her on the ground, when she got on the ground, she was so pretty and so nice-looking, they didn't want to send the basket back to get the other guy. They wanted him to stay there. They didn't want to get him up.

So anyhow, he was waiting for the basket to come down. No basket. Nobody was around to help him out. So he started going around in that hole— the hole was so big—he started to go around the hole. First thing he met, he met the place where there were all kinds of cattle, animals, a funny kind. Cows and bulls and all kinds, horses, and all kinds of stuff underneath there. So he didn't want to bother too much there, he kept on, he was looking around. He found a place where there were all kinds of wagons, and cripes knows what was in there. So he said to himself, "It must be in this building somewhere."

He met that Beast with Seven Heads. So, she was just going around the room where he was, trying to get him. But every time she used to fasten him, he used to hit her with his cane, and cut a head off. So he cut the seven heads off the beast. And when the head was gone, he took his knife. And he took their tongues, of the seven heads, and he put them in his pocket—put the tongues in his pocket.

So, he kept on walking. And when he got far enough, he met an eagle, a big eagle. So he wanted to talk to the eagle, and he said to the eagle, he said, "Have you any chance for me to be climbing up the hole again, going up on the ground once more?" She said, "No. The only thing I can tell you—I can take you up myself. But you've got to have a quarter meat to throw in my beak every time I flap my wings, in order to go up."

So he said, "That's no trouble. If she wants to take me up, I'll get that."

So he went where he had found the cattle and things like that. He killed so many of them,

182

and he dragged them below the hole, cut them by pieces, and he got it ready.

So, the eagle came and took him. And every time she was flapping her wings, he used to throw a quarter beef in her beak. So, she got him up there. A quarter of beef, in her beak. So she got up there. Well, after he got up there, he hauled up his basket and he put it there.

So, he left for the place where the king was living. He went at the palace where the king was. And they were just getting ready to get married. Brise-Bois and that girl were ready to get married, see. So when he went there, he went to the king and he told him, he said, "I thought it was the guy that had saved your daughter that was going to marry your daughter."

Well, the king didn't know any better. The king said, "Yes." He said, "That's what it is. It's the guy that saved my daughter that's getting married today."

He said, "Did you ever ask your daughter if it was the right guy?" But she didn't know exactly herself, she didn't know one from the others, you know? She didn't really know their name or face or anything, just that she knew it was one of them.

He said, "Yes, and she said it was him."

He said, "Did you ever give anything to your daughter for a souvenir or a present or things like that?"

So the king tried to remember. So he said, "Yes, I did. I gave her a handkerchief, with those

183

three different apples in it—an orange, gold, and a silver apple."

"If a guy would show you those gifts, will you believe it's him that saved your daughter?"

He said, "Yes."

He said, "Your daughter never told you that there were three men that were looking after her. Were passing there three times a day, and looking after her so nobody would steal her."

"Oh," he said, "yes, she told me that."

He said, "She never told you there was a beast, a Seven-Headed Beast that was passing there once a day, that was looking after her, anybody'll touch her."

He said, "Yes, I know—she told me that."

He said, "If a man showed you the seven tongues from the seven heads, will you believe it's him that saved your daughter?"

"Oh," he said, "I would, all right, because it's nothing but the truth if you've got them."

So he put his hand in his pocket and he hauled out the tongues and he showed it to him. And the handkerchief with the apples. So he said, "Now I believe it's you." He said, "They're getting ready to get married." He said, "What are we going to do with them?"

He said, "There's not much you can do with it. You can put one of them to feed the pigs, and the other one to feed the chickens." He said, "I'm the one that's going to marry her, going to marry the daughter."

184

So at that time I came home—I didn't want to stay there any longer.

It's the best I can do in English.

(Do you remember when you first heard this story?) Oh, I remember I was only young.

This was an old man that was staying not too far from here, across the beach there. And in those days there was no place to go—no dance, no shows, nor anything to go. But to try and gather at a place like that, tell stories, and hear something like that. And we used to go there quite often, just to hear the stories. Because he knew all kinds of stories. Joe Boudreau. He was a blind man. Oh, you could have been there two or three days, always telling different stories.

Sid Timmons: Stories from the Coal Pit

I went in the mine when I was ten and a half, and I trapped a door for two days. That's opening and closing the door for the horses going in and out— the doors are for ventilation.

On the third day, one of the drivers got hurt—got a bolt stuck in his foot. So—I was used to a horse around home—so naturally I volunteered that I'd drive. And, foolish enough, they gave me the horse.

And I always remember the first horse. His name was Diamond—one eye.

And if you spit in his face, he'd follow you around all day till he got a chance to rub it off on you.

He wouldn't bite you or anything, but just follow around—and rub it off.

Oh, yes.

•

In the week's pay—the overman would make up the pay—well, if you unloaded a box of timber, you got 46 cents.

That all went in as consideration. Timber and consideration. You know. Was no set rate—it would cover a multitude of sins.

So, if you and I were working together, the only difference in your pay would be a ton of coal.

The ton was never split in two. This week you got the extra ton, and I got it next week. If there was an odd ton—you know. That was the only difference in our pays, was the odd ton.

But anyhow, you and I got our pay—and you'd always compare them—you know. We'd have the same, clear of that.

This fellow drew his pay and he had ten dollars over, and his buddy said to him, "How come, boy, you got ten dollars? You didn't work any extra time."

"No. But," he said, "I sold a cow to the overman, for ninety dollars. And," he said, "he's paying me ten dollars a week for nine weeks."

Consideration.

He said, "That's fine. He's got to pay me, too, or I'm going to squeal on him."

So the coal company paid a hundred and eighty dollars for the cow.

•

But I had a dog. He was what they call a badger hound. And he'd tackle anything—didn't matter how big it was—anything. And he'd stay with it. He didn't know what it was to back off.

But anyhow, I was on the back shift all alone, so I decided to take him to the pit with me. You know—good company.

So, I took him. And the first night, he got a rat. He grabbed the rat by the head—like that. And when he grabbed the rat, the rat grabbed his tongue. I had to kill the rat in his mouth.

But he never made that mistake after. He could kill them.

But anyhow, he'd be with me all night. And while he didn't have a check number—that was all right— he knew every move, you know.

So the first day I was day shift, Monday morning, I said to my wife, "Don't let this dog out till at least half past seven."

Now, where I was going to work in the mine, he had never been down there. And there was a door. He'd have to wait for the door to be opened to get through—you know.

187

My brother and another fellow were rum sick. And about nine o'clock, this thing passed, you know.

The other fellow said to my brother, he said, "Boy," he said, "I was drinking, but," he said, "I never saw a rat that big in my life. Did you see that?"

And my brother said, "Yeah. But it wasn't a rat. I don't think. Couldn't be," he said, "that big."

The dog—he was only about that high, but he was about that long, you know.

Well, it scared the two of them, you know. They thought they were in the jigs then.

And he came down. And at ten o'clock that dog found me. He waited till someone opened the door, and he shot through it. And he was never down there before. Yeah.

That's the day I got mad at him and I put him on a full trip of coal and sent him up—to see if he'd be killed?

And Francis MacEachern said, when the trip stopped on the surface—he'd just dug a little hole in the corner of the box. He jumped off and shook himself and went out to the washhouse.

He was there when I came up in the evening.

•

The pit stopped hoisting coal by night—just what empty boxes were there, you'd get them. So, course, him and his buddy had preference over me and my brother. We were driving two places, and of course they were in the main place—they got the preference, you know.

So, the day shift shotfirer came up and he said, "Sid, no use in you going down tonight. There's only fourteen empties." So, we'd need thirteen or fourteen a pair. He said, "That's all we got. So," he said, "the other fellows get the preference."

I said, "They won't tonight, boy."

So my brother said, "Let's go home."

I said, "No, we're not going home."

And, as you go down in the slope—there's about 200 feet of concrete slope—there'd be worms on it. And they'd be as blue—and thin, you know. No nourishment.

I picked two or three of these worms. And I knew that my wife had put sausage in my lunch, you know. So, I made sure to sit with him.

And we had another thousand feet to go— from nine to ten. And I said, "Look, Ranald, before I get out of the rig I'm going to have a bite to eat."

I had the worms all the time, you know. They were getting pretty lively then in my hand.

I took some of the sausage out and chewed it up, and started to cough. Spit it in my hand where the worms were. I said, "Look. . . ."

There was a squirt of vomit came out of that fellow, boy. He vomited all over the fellow in front of him.

When the rake stopped he said to his buddy, "Let's go home. I can't work." And they went home.

My brother and I got the boxes. Yeah.

Many's the time I made him sick.

●

They got—well, they had two—but they got this third mule, and they couldn't get her down into the mine. So, he came along to me one evening and he said, "How about taking that mule down?" And I said, "All right."

So, I went out eleven o'clock that night. Instead of taking her down, I took her up on the bankhead. You know—it was steep. And my father and—there were seven old fellows—big fellows. So, I got them to push her, till I got below the concrete. Well, the minute I got below the concrete, she was all right, you know.

I took her down. I spent two weeks with her on the back shift—alone. Breaking her in. I got her down pretty good.

But she never moved till I'd get in the box. And I never had to speak to her. The minute I stepped on the box, she was gone.

But anyhow, this day they brought an efficiency expert, and—they were touring the mine. There was the superintendent and the head engineer—general super—our manager (he was very sarcastic) and the underground manager.

And we had a fellow by the name of John Alec Brown. Aw, he was a character. He could jig a tune—you'd swear to God it was coming right out of a violin, you know.

And there was a violin player two thousand

feet above. So, John Alec had heard a tune, and he called up this violin player, you know. He wanted to know if he had it right.

And he was jigging the tune for him over the telephone. All alone.

When all these officials came down and they opened the door—right below, they could hear this music, you know. Fellow going at it with the phone.

So anyhow, they came in. And I was standing, with the mule hooked on. And when I'd go in (I'd take four boxes in), after she passed four box lengths, she knew herself. She'd just stop, you know—and start backing out on the other road.

I never had to—I'd jump off and let her pass. Then I'd shift the track. Never had to speak to her at all.

So, they came along. And the manager said, "There's one of your American pit horses." You know. So the underground manager said, "Yes. And a hell of a lot of good—she's good for nothing."

So, just as they went to pass, I stepped on the box. And I crowed like a rooster—you know. I knew the mare—she'd go anyway. And she left.

So I stopped on the way in and I let them pass. When I figured they were just about into the inside of the road, I went in. And I jumped off. And the minute the fourth box passed, I started grunting like a pig. She backed right out, you know.

And I hooked her off and went out.

We were passing the office that evening. The

manager called me in, and this other fellow.

He said, "We went down there today," he said. "And we had strangers with us. And when we opened the deep door, you'd think," he said, "there was an orchestra down there. And what was it but one God damn fool," he said, "jigging a tune with two sticks.

"And," he said, "we went in on the landing. And I thought we ran into a God damn menagerie," he said. "There were more animals running loose in there."

He said, "If I hadda had a maul—I'd have hit you two fellows in the forehead."

He was embarrassed, you know.

He came in one day, and this Brown was jigging a tune with two sticks.

Fellow by the name of Tomerey had his pants off—and he had a pair of gum shoes on the wrong feet. And we had an old trapdoor—and he was step-dancing.

And there were two fellows boxing, and I was refereeing. And I was supposed to be boss—road boss.

Boy.

See, we had no overman over us.

We were doing our work. We'd run like hell to get our work done—then wait—while we were waiting, see.

Boy, that was a bad day that day. And I ended up on the receiving end on account of being kind of in charge.

Them times, everybody tried to make a dollar.

But there was deep-down friendship with everybody, you know.

And there was a lot of friendly rivalry. Even a man that hated you, like, you know—if anything happened to you—you were injured or anything— he'd be the first man there to help.

And, if you weren't hurt bad he'd say, "It's a pity you weren't killed."

•

And then, the pair of men above—you always tried to beat them. The same as in the woods—you tried to beat them a couple of logs. Well, in the mine you liked to beat them a box of coal. If possible.

You know, it wasn't the thought of the money—it was just that you loaded a ton more than the other fellow.

Of course, that's why there's so many old Cape Bretoners today all bent and crippled. You know, the Cape Bretoner had—he had to be tougher. He had to be able to drink more rum than anyone else. You know. He had to be able to fight better than anyone else. And he had to be able to load coal and cut logs and lift better than anyone else. And a lot of them, to prove it, injured themselves.

•

Well, they claim the company got forty dollars for a man and fifty dollars for a horse—insurance.

I don't know if that was true or not—that's what they claim.

See, this is why, if you were breaking in horses they'd say to you, "If you can't work him, kill him."

'Cause they couldn't get fifty dollars for a bad horse when you'd come up. The word'd get around the horse was no good, and nobody'd buy him.

Generally sold for twenty-five dollars or so.

•

But there was quite an attachment for a boy and his horse in the mine, you know. Like, a lot of them, they became attached to their horse very much. Some of them—if their horse got killed— they'd cry just like it was their mother, you know.

Yeah, some of them never went back. They wouldn't go back driving any more, if they lost their horse.

Home-Brew on Sunday!

by Josie Matheson Bredbury

(*Josie, tell me about what happened to that cow. What's the story behind that cow?*) Well, she lived!

(*But I mean, what happened there?*) Well, they made the home-brew. There was John Murdock and Johnny and my brother Jimmy. And there was another one—I really can't remember who the other guy was. But he wasn't with them all the time. But those three boys (made) the stuff from the house, and took the stuff out in the pasture, and put it in this wooden washtub my mother had. And they had a wooden top to put on it— boards, you know.

So they put it out there. I don't know what they put in it. Except that they had hot water— boiling water. I guess there was—I don't know if there was yeast, but anyway....

(*They made a home-brew.*) Oh, yeah. They filled up the tub out there. (*They'd put it out there to brew...?*) Yeah, because my father, you know, would kill them (for) doing it.

So, the minister came that day—it was a Sunday at that. And my mother, you know, she'd let them do anything. All the women would, you know, those days. So we told the minister—A. C. (Archie) Fraser—"Take Papa for two or three days"—with

195

him. Because the boys wanted to do this. So Archie said, "What are you girls up to this time?" Every time we'd tell him to take Papa, we were going to paper the house or do something, you know.

So anyway, he took Papa. And the boys got busy right away.

And then a day or two after that, we missed a cow. And she didn't have horns. And we called her "Maoli." So, we couldn't find her high and low, the pasture there. So, down in the corner of the pasture, it's swampy. So Jimmy thought, "Well, I'll go down there. She might have got caught in the mud down there." So he did, and he couldn't find her down there.

So on his way back, he thought, "Well, I guess I'll look at the brew"—whatever they called it. So he went up there. And here was the cow, stiff as a poker on the ground. He thought she was dead, at first. So he took his handkerchief off his neck and put it up her nose and she went, "Wooof!" So he knew she was living, anyway.

So then he wrestled around getting the boys with him. I wasn't there. But they got the cow on her feet, anyway. And they took her away out in the pasture, away from the house.

So, Papa was supposed to come home. And they kept walking her around and around and around. I guess—is that what they do to drunks? (*Josie laughed.*)

So anyway, he was doing okay. And they left her out there anyway. And, oh, I don't know if we milked her that day—I guess somebody milked her out there. But when she came in with the other cows, they were milking her for two or three days. And nothing came but foam! From the moo! (*Laughter.*)

Oh, Lord. It was really comical. My poor mother, she was laughing at them. So she told them, "Now, you did that on Sunday. You shouldn't have done it on Sunday." (*Laughter.*) "That's why the cow ate it all up." She ate the whole thing! She swept the whole thing out!

I guess there was a lot more to it, you know, that I can't—I wasn't with them out there. We had to stay at the house to keep an eye on Papa when he'd come home.

(*Did you ever taste the brew?*) No. No.... There was nothing left to be tasted! Although they made other batches. They made one—about the hens....

They made that one in the barn. I think it was the same boys. It must have been. It was on a Sunday, too. Everything was done on a Sunday, because Papa would be reading, and we could keep an eye on him—he'd be in the other room, you know. Then they'd be doing this. And if Papa'd move, we'd run and tell the boys!

Anyway, this day, they made it in the barn, I think, this time. It was a smaller batch. And, however, was it a week, or how many days—they thought they'd taste it. And nobody'd taste it because they were afraid it'd poison them. So they

197

wouldn't taste it. Well, they thought, well—here Mama was letting the hens out in the late afternoon. And we had the porch on the back of the house at that time, and we always sat out there, evening. So anyway, they thought, well, they'd put it in—she had one of those wooden crocks, to put water in for the hens. So the boys put the stuff in the hens' crock.

So, we were out in the back sitting down, Sunday evening. And who came around the front of the house and around the side of the house, like this, was the rooster. And he couldn't crow, and his wings were out like this, balancing himself! (*Josie is laughing.*) Oh, God, it was funny. I'm telling you, it was so funny. We were all out there— Mama and Papa, and Jimmy and Roddy were with us that day. And the hens—there were about twelve hens behind him. And the rooster would go—(*Josie makes the sounds of hiccups and failed hoarse crowing*)—and he couldn't crow at all. And the hens behind—(*the sounds of drunken clucking*). And every one of them was balancing with their wings.

Papa turned to Mama and he said to her, "Effie, what happened to the hens?" (*The sounds of the rooster and hens*)—you know. And the boys took off, through the house. They knew what happened. They knew what had happened—they'd given it to the hens instead of...!

Oh, my golly, I'm telling you—those two incidents, I never could forget. We girls got up and

198

swooshed them away from us so Papa wouldn't see them any more. Oh, golly. But my mother knew what happened.

(*Your mother was lenient.*) Oh, yes. Yeah, she was wonderful. She'd let them do anything, and let us do anything, too, you know. She'd always— she used to say—of course she'd say it in Gaelic, and it sounded funnier in Gaelic—"I'm not in this with you." She'd always say, "I'm not in this with you." God bless her....

Joe Neil MacNeil and Treasure Hunting

There was one place, we were very suspicious of it. There was a boulder of granite and there were no other granite boulders round in that area. And there was a fairly large stone down there and it had been cut away, and there was just a fairly large piece left in the centre the full length of it— forming a cross on the stone. It wasn't cut into the stone, but the rest of the stone was gone—like it was chiseled away or weathered, but this centre was raised a little bit, maybe a quarter of an inch or so. And the old man told us about this and of course we thought we'd find out if there was anything there. I tried it with the witch-hazel divining rod and I found there was some mineral there anyway. And another fellow who used to go with us, he tried and he said there was something there anyway. There was a big boulder over—not the one the cross was on—this was a boulder left down there—and we blasted that, put a charge in it and split the boulder and had it moved away from there, and we were digging underneath that for part of the night—but we never got down to the chest or whatever was there.

Of course, treasures have been found, wherever they came from. A treasure was found out in Richmond County. A girl was working at a certain place and she saw a box, part of a box sticking out of the clay bank on the shore. And she came home and she told the merchants about seeing this box—it looked like a box anyway. So one day they went there, and they found the box with some treasure in it—there was silver or gold or some jewels or something in it. The story was that they gave her a dress—the merchants could well afford to give her a new dress as a reward for telling them she had seen it. I guess they made a good profit.

There was a lady telling me that her husband and two or three others went to an island— that was up in Richmond County, one of the islands. They went out supposed to dig, going working on a buried treasure, and they went over at night to the island. And they started to dig down there. And all of a sudden a storm came up—

thunder and lightning and wind, and one of them said, "We'd better make it for home. The women will be dead thinking of us out here in this weather." So they made for the shore and went down and pushed the boat off the shore and they had only gone maybe 100 yards or 200 yards from shore—the storm was over. They came home and one of the women said, "My, you people didn't stay long." Her husband said, "No, of course we didn't stay long. We weren't going to stay in that storm. You people would be worried about us." "What do you mean," she said, "worried about you?" He said, "Didn't you have a terrible thunder storm?" "No," she said, "we didn't have a storm of any kind all night."

Up in Richmond County, they were digging at this place and they figured they were getting pretty close to whatever was there—and they heard a queer scream and cawing and when they looked, the area was covered with crows from where they were as far down along as they could see—there was nothing but crows. "Let's forget about it, we won't bother with this any more." And down at Big Pond Centre—there were fellows down there digging—and the man who told me, I'm sure he was pretty truthful about it—said that they left. Said that the crows got so bad you couldn't hear anything, screaming, every tree around had a bunch of crows on it and it was just like they were going wild. And no cause for it because they weren't disturbing anything. The crows when they were on the trees at night were roosting, but no, those were crowing and screaming and screetching around—and the fellow said, "Let's leave, we'll forget about it." Two different places where the crows had chased them.

From Billy James MacNamara...

Another story I used to hear my grandfather telling here, about some old woman around here some years ago—they had her kind of suspected as a witch. So. Her next-door neighbour used to get milk from her—get a bottle of milk—they didn't have any cows. Get a bottle of milk from her. So this evening she went over to her house. And (the old woman) said, "The cows never got home tonight. They're in the woods, and I couldn't hunt them. But," she said, "you wait. I'll get you a bottle of milk." She said, "Give me your bottle." She ran to the rocking chair—a big chair she had, a big setting chair. And she had a gimlet, one of those awls, bored a hole in it, and held the thing under it—and the milk poured out and filled her quart of milk for her! Made a hole under the rocking chair and held a bottle under it and filled it with milk. She was a real witch then.

D. W. and the Bear

by Margaret & Frank MacRae

Margaret: Do you know any of Donald William's stories?

Frank: Oh, the only story that I know, that D.W. told—the time he was out trapping out in the woods, during winter. He came home. And he was telling the story. And they were talking how cold it was last night. Oh, he said, it was terrible cold where he was last night—that the light in the lamp froze! The kerosene lamp, you know—that it was so cold that the flame froze.

Margaret: He was great at telling stories like that, you know, just to be funny, and people used to get a kick out of them.

He used to make up these stories—they were just lies, you know. He used to make them up for fun, just to entertain people. He loved to entertain them. People who would gather like that in a house in the evening. D.W. was there—that would be the entertainment for the evening, D.W. telling stories that he made up.

He was telling one time about the bear, when he got him on the pole of the wagon.

He was hauling supplies out to the Oregon *(a pulp-cutting operation at St. Ann's Bay)* when the Oregon was working. And he was going out with a load, a big wagon full of supplies. And he was on his way out, halfways up the mountain—here he met this big bear ahead of him on the road. And oh, he didn't know what he was going to do.

The bear stood his ground. He didn't know what he was going to do. He didn't have a gun or anything. But he had a cask of molasses on the load, along with the other supplies.

So he took the horses out of the wagon—the wagon had a pole between the two horses, you know—and he tied them to the back of the wagon. And he knocked the bung out of the keg of molasses and he smeared the pole with molasses. The bear started licking the pole and eating the pole. And as he was going along, the pole was going down his throat. Finally the pole came out on the other end. And he put the pin in it, and he had him—the bear tied to the pole!

Well, the people would listen to that and laugh to kill themselves!

Frank: Oh, he was great to pass time, you know. (*What was D.W.'s last name?*) **Margaret:** MacLeod. He lived out in West Tarbot. D.W.'d come in and he'd sit and tell stories. He was as happy as a lark. There was nobody happier than he was. Anywhere. He raised his family, and they grew up, and they survived.

Archie Neil Tells the Story of Piper's Glen

told by Archie Neil Chisholm

This is another story that has its beginning on the Island of Barra in Scotland and has its ending at Piper's Glen where John Archie MacKenzie came from. It goes back to the early days in Barra where a woman lost her husband and she had two young boys growing up. And in the meantime not too far away a man had become a widower and he had one son. He and the widow married so they had the three children—two of the widow's sons, and one of his.

The man would have to go out fishing to make a living, and he would be out all the time and the lady he married was quite mean to her stepson. But the man didn't know it and the little boy wouldn't tell him very much. But one of the things that she would do was to have her two boys well trained and as graceful and gracious as possible. They learned how to play the pipes when they were very young and they would not allow their stepbrother to touch the pipes. He had a little tin whistle and he used to go out and play the tin whistle and he would play beautifully on the tin whistle. But they wouldn't listen to him or anything like that.

So according to tradition the boy was out

alone one day in some barren place and he was
playing on his little tin whistle and all of a sudden
he noticed a little man standing in front of him.
And he stopped playing and the little man told
him, "Don't be afraid of me," he said. "You would
like to learn to play the pipes." And the little fellow said, "Yes, I would." And he said, "I want you
to do something, and don't be afraid. I want you to
put your right hand in my mouth, and when I nod
my head, take your hand out of my mouth and put
your left hand in." And the young fellow did that
and just as he did, this little man disappeared.

But the strangest thing about it was that the
young fellow started to play the tin whistle again,
and this time he could do anything with it. He was
getting the most beautiful sounds out of it. So he
figured, I've got to learn to play the pipes. And one
day when the mother was gone and the two boys
were gone with her, he took one of their sets of
pipes and he learned that he could play the most
beautiful music in the world on it. But they didn't
know anything about it.

Now, we leave them there and we go to another part of Barra where a man had decided—he
had a nice sailing vessel—and he decided that he
was going to start making trips between the islands, between Barra and Lewis and all the He-
brides. He wanted a piper to play, and he was going from one place to the other looking for pipers.
And he landed at this house one day and the
mother proudly presented her two boys and they

both played the pipes. And then he asked, "What about him?" "Oh, he can't play." Well the little fellow said, "Let me try." And he played, he played beautifully and the man hired him.

So that was fine. They travelled, he was playing as an entertainer on the boat. The man bought him a new set of pipes and everything. That went on for about two years and then the owner of the schooner decided that he was going to sail for America and he took the young fellow with him.

They sailed across the Atlantic and they were off the coast of Halifax, so many miles off what they call Sambro Light or someplace like that— and they were becalmed. You see, you depended on the wind for everything. And there wasn't a pocket full of wind to be had. The boat was there and suddenly they discovered that the boat was taking on water, that she was leaking some place. They knew they had to get help or something and the captain didn't know what to do. The young fellow said to him, "I have magic in my pipes. I will send a message out and somebody will get it."

Well, the captain paid no attention to him. He figured, You crazy little fella, but go ahead. And the young fellow played, and strange as it seems, somewhere probably twenty miles away somebody who understood was supposed to have heard the signal, the S.O.S., the signal, and he began to tell his neighbours that there was a boat in distress. And they sailed out from the coast off the Halifax shore someplace and they found the boat

207

and they found the crew and saved them. They towed the schooner into Halifax.

But one of the things the boy swore to himself, he thought: If ever I get off this boat I will never go to sea again. And, he said, I'm going to get as far from the sea as I can.

And he left Halifax with his pipes and his little duffel bag and he walked and came across the Strait (of Canso) and came to Cape Breton Island. And he came as far inland as possible, and landed in a heavily wooded area and he said, "This is the place where I'll stay." And he built a little log cabin for himself.

And after a couple of years he got more acquainted in the area and he found a wife for himself and he got married and they had a great, large family. And each of them was taught to play the pipes. Men and women. And their names were Jamiesons, they were James's sons. And it was from the name of this Jamieson family who were all such beautiful pipers that the place up there received the name of Piper's Glen.

How the Old Man Kept His Stories Alive

told by Dan Hughie MacIsaac

There were two fellows made a bet, up at my grandfather's place. This is the truth now. Up at my grandfather's place. Made a bet who would tell the longest story.

Well, when he came to the house, he turned around and he says, "The man that came here to tell the longest story is the first to tell it." So they started about nine o'clock. It came to twelve o'clock and the story was going. It came to three o'clock and the story was going. And it came morning, and the story was going. And he followed him down to the road, still telling the story!

He never got a chance to tell his story—the other fellow was putting more and more and more to it!

I'll tell you a funny story. There was a fellow up— and it's the truth. An old fellow was walking up the road, up by Port Ban or Sight Point. And anyways, he was staying with a couple. He was an old fellow and he was staying with a couple there.

So anyways, there was a little gate to go up to the house, and there was a big gate where they take the wagons in. And they saw him coming. And he passed by the gate. By gosh, they didn't know what to say. He kept on, and he passed by the big gate. And he kept on going. And he was awhile away, and they were getting kind of uneasy about it.

So finally they saw him coming back. And he came up to the house. And John Alex was the name of the guy that was looking after him. He says, "What happened to you today?"

"How?"

"You passed the two gates and you kept on going."

"Well, I'll just tell you what happened to me. I was telling myself a story, and I wasn't through with it, and I had to keep on going till I finished!"

(*Dan Hughie laughs.*) Till he finished the story he was telling himself!

continued on next page . . .